350/B

W9-CHL-818

JOEL IS THE YOUNGEST
by
Judith Ish-Kishor
Illustrated by Jules Gotlieb

Joel remembered Hanukkah last year, when he was seven. His brothers and sisters lit candles ahead of him, but now that he was eight, his father let him light the Shammos, the important middle candle, so he felt good. But in many other ways, he felt left out of the activities of his older brothers. When they moved into a new house, Joel was allowed to have his own room. He spent so much time with his Grandfather that they became close friends and from him Joel learned stories of the Jewish holidays and of the Hebrew men who were important in American history. Joel wrote them into plays for family entertainment and when Brotherhood Week was celebrated, his plays were put on for the whole school. But it took more than that to prove to his older brothers that he was catching up, and this was an exciting adventure all his own!

* * * *

Dewey Decimal Classification: F

About the Author:

JUDITH ISH-KISHOR was born in Boston, brought up in London, returned to the United States for her last year of high school, then attended Hunter College. She began telling stories when she was only six, to keep her brothers and sisters quiet. She was the eldest of eight children, so remembered the struggles of the younger ones sufficiently to write *Joel is the Youngest*. She lives in New York City.

About the Illustrator:

JULES GOTLIEB was born in New York City, but he and his wife now live in the country. At sixteen, he had a studio and did posters and landscapes. By the time he was nineteen he was art director for a lithography firm. The Gotliebs have traveled in Europe, North Africa, the West Indies, South America and the jungles of Dutch Guiana, always finding much to sketch.

JOEL IS THE YOUNGEST

by JUDITH ISH-KISHOR

Illustrated

by Jules Gotlieb

1964 FIRST CADMUS EDITION
THIS SPECIAL EDITION IS PUBLISHED BY ARRANGEMENT WITH
THE PUBLISHERS OF THE REGULAR EDITION
JULIAN MESSNER, INC.
BY

E. M. HALE AND COMPANY
EAU CLAIRE, WISCONSIN

JU
F
Is 3
b

Copyright 1954 by Judith Ish-Kishor

Library of Congress Catalog Card No. 54-10587

This edition lithographed in U. S. A. by Wetzel Bros., Inc., Milwaukee 2, Wisconsin

20   1-31-67   SSG   3.50

To

my little friend

SAMUEL LEVINGER

who grew up to be

a hero

Contents

JOEL IS THE YOUNGEST

CHAPTER ONE

THE BIRTHDAY PARTY

Potatoes are not the most interesting things to be sent for. Joel could think of pleasanter jobs than walking five blocks to the store where Mother bought her vegetables. But now that he had the scooter-wagon it was different. Since Phil had made it for him, hammering it together out of a soapbox, an old plank and a roller skate that had come apart, Joel knew that any errand can be fun!

He lowered the potato bag into the wagon, set his right foot on the shaft and with one push flew along the sidewalk. He could pretend he was a motorman, taking his train around a curve, or the driver of a fire engine. Whenever he had to slow down, he could be an early settler guiding a covered wagon over the Western plains.

This time, however, his make-believe stopped as he passed a candy and stationery store. He was himself again—Joel, age eight, and the youngest of a family of four. He gazed at the jigsaw puzzle in

the window and knew he had found the perfect
present for Phil's birthday.

A hundred little, queerly curved pieces made up
a picture of big, handsome horses, all brown or
spotted gray and white. One was drinking from a
pond. Another was rearing up while a farmer held
him by the cheek-strap. A third was nibbling at
grass in the shade of some trees.

Joel hadn't been able to thank Phil enough for
the scooter, but this present would show how grate-
ful he felt. Philip liked puzzles. Besides, this would

make a good big package—not at all the kind of thing he'd expect from "the kid." Most important of all, the price had come down from a dollar to seventy-five cents. Joel thought he should be able to raise that much between now and Philip's birthday.

Joel didn't buy the ice-cream cone he wanted. Instead he rushed home with the scooter, to count the money in his bank.

Mother had given him an empty syrup bottle shaped like a bear sitting up on its hind legs. He dropped his money through a slot in the metal top. Joel unscrewed the cap and spread his savings on the kitchen table.

It had looked like a lot. Now he saw that it was mostly pennies. He had forty-four cents. He put in the "lucky penny" he had found in the street one day. That made it forty-five cents.

Mother asked him what he was excited about. He knew Mother could keep a secret, so he told her. "Do you want me to hold the money for you, while you save?" she asked.

"Yes!" said Joel quickly. He remembered how pleasant and easy Mother had made it for him last year. In his heart, however, he knew she must have added some coins herself, so that he shouldn't be too short of candy and spending money.

Maybe a boy of seven did need her help. But now he was eight. That made it different. "No, thanks, Mom," he said. "I have to do this all by myself. What's half of thirty cents?"

"Fifteen."

"Oh yes, of course." That meant he would have to save fifteen cents from his allowance next week and the week after. That would leave ten cents a week for other things.

It gave him a feeling of great satisfaction to add a dime and a nickel to the mostly brown pile inside the bear. Joel smiled as he did so, knowing that Phil would be both surprised and pleased.

Then Joel went into his usual daydream. What must it feel like to be eleven, as Philip would be on his birthday? Of course it was even grander for Alex, who was past thirteen and the eldest in the family. But Joel would be content to change places with Phil.

He bought himself ten cents' worth of sourballs, and spaced them out, two a day, making each one last as long as he could. But they were always finished too soon!

Meanwhile, since he couldn't afford a birthday card, Sally, who was ten years old, showed him how to make one. She was very good at drawing.

Sally came next to Joel in the Mendoza family, and sometimes she made him angry by siding with the two older boys when they treated him like a baby.

Today Sally was kind and understanding. She

gave Joel a sheet of paper from her drawing pad and told him to fold it in half. Then, when he was about to cut into the dust cover of *Bambi*, to paste the picture of the little deer onto the front of the birthday card, Sally stopped him.

"You don't have to spoil that," she said. Spreading some tracing paper over the picture, she gave him a sharp pencil with which to trace Bambi's outline. She showed him how to use carbon paper in transferring the outline to the birthday card, and lent him her best crayons.

Joel colored the picture of Bambi light brown, with some dark streaks and spots. On the inside page he printed:

To Phil
Wishing him Many Happy Returns
Joel

Each word was in a different color. Mother found him a large square envelope, and the card was ready.

On the day that Joel brought his money to the store, the puzzle was gone from the window. His heart sank. He told himself that it might not be sold. Perhaps they had only taken it inside. He hurried into the store. Mrs. Silver was behind the counter.

"Where's the puzzle that was in the window? The one with the horses?" he asked breathlessly.

"It's sold," she told him. "But we have others."

Joel groaned in his disappointment. "That was a nice hard one. I wanted it for my brother Phil."

"Cheer up!" said Mrs. Silver. "I think I have another one that you'll like." She looked at several boxes on the shelf, and took one down. "This is 'A Scene in the Nation's Capital,'" she read. "'The Jefferson Memorial, Washington, D. C.'"

The cover showed a long row of cherry trees, their masses of pink and white blossoms reflected in blue water. On the further side of the water you could see a white building with a stately dome.

"Yes, I like that," said Joel. "Thanks." While Mrs. Silver wrapped the puzzle, he laid his money on the counter. She picked it up, the silver pieces first, and left a nickel and a penny on the counter.

"What's the matter? Did I count it wrong?" asked Joel.

"No. The price has gone down again. It's only sixty-nine cents."

"Then I can have an ice-cream cone!" Joel exclaimed gleefully.

He bought a strawberry cone and ate it on the way home. It tasted all the better because he had gone without one for so long.

The birthday arrived. Joel, who liked school most of the time, thought it would never be over, that day. He was so impatient for suppertime and the party! He couldn't wait to hear what they would say about his present.

As always at their birthday parties, no outsiders were invited—just the family and it was the birthday child who chose what they would have for supper.

The table looked beautiful, with a pale yellow cloth and a bunch of purple asters in the center. In front of Phil's place, at Mother's right hand, was a pile of birthday cards. Some of them had come by mail that morning, but he hadn't opened any.

Joel sat down facing Philip and next to Mother. Alex and Sally took the seats beside Father. Joel felt a thrill of happiness. This was the most wonderful moment of all!

Phil was opening the envelopes and looking at the birthday cards. A funny one from aunt Millie opened out larger and larger, until it was nearly the size of a tablecloth. A cowboy swung a lasso across Alex's card, yelling "Yippee!" There was an orchid on Sally's card, and a big "11" in blue and gold on Mother's.

Out of a large square envelope Philip took Joel's card and studied it a moment. "Look at this!" he exclaimed, holding it up so they could see both the little deer and the many-colored greeting inside. "From Joel! He made it himself."

Sally nodded wisely. Joel laughed. Everybody wanted to see that card and they passed it from hand to hand. Looking across at Joel, Phil said: "Gee! Thanks! That's a swell one!"

Joel thought happily: What will he think of the *present?*

He looked around the table, almost as if he were seeing his folks for the first time. Alex, the eldest, was the boy who looked like Father, with gray eyes and light hair. Phil had gray eyes too; but he and Joel had Mother's dark hair, except that hers was wavy and neat and theirs was usually rumpled. Sally didn't look like any of them, with her fluffy brown hair and blue eyes.

"Supper!" cried Father. "Or I'll take a bite out of Joel's card!" Phil rescued it and arranged the cards on a shelf.

Mother and Father took up their spoons and began on the grapefruit. The older children helped themselves to sugar. Phil passed the bowl to Joel, who said suddenly: "No thanks." He had decided to eat the grapefruit without it, as their parents were doing. It gave him the feeling of being quite grown-up.

Phil's favorite dish was pot roast cooked with potatoes and carrots in plenty of gravy. Mother filled their plates while Father poured ginger ale into their glasses.

He raised his glass, looking toward Phil, and they did the same. "Here's to Philip!" said Father. "May he have many happy returns of today!" They drank.

"Thanks!" said Phil, blushing. He blushed

easily. Joel took a long drink from his glass. The bubbles tickled his throat. He giggled.

Joel's eyes wandered to the row of presents on the side table near the wall. They were arranged in the order of the giver's age, with Father's at one end and Joel's at the other.

"You know," Alex remarked, "Father's package is a small one, this time, and Joel's is big. Isn't that funny?"

"Yes. I'm dying to know what's in Joel's," said Phil. Joel laughed, rocking forward on his seat with delight.

"Anyone can tell what mine is," said Sally. She gazed regretfully at the longish narrow parcel next to Joel's. "I just couldn't think of anything else."

"But I need a new tie," said Phil, "and you've got good taste. I know it won't be sky-blue pink with flowers all over it."

"*Mine's* sky-blue pink with flowers all over it!" Joel said mysteriously.

"Whatever can it be?" cried Mother as if she didn't know.

"Wait and see," sang Joel. This was even more fun than he had expected.

For dessert they had baked apples with chopped raisins and nuts in place of the core.

Now it was time for the birthday cake. Mother carried it in, all glowing with lighted candles, as

they sang "Happy Birthday." "Eleven candles," she said as she set it down, "and one for good measure!"

What a fine show they made! Joel remembered how bare his cake had looked with only eight candles. Phil blew out the little flames and Mother cut the cake and began passing it around.

"Eleven! How wonderful!" said Joel and Sally in one breath. Then they linked their little fingers and kept silent, to get a "wish."

"Alex is past thirteen," Philip reminded them modestly.

"Still we'd like to be—" Joel stopped. But it was too late. Whoever spoke first lost his wish.

"I get my wish!" cried Sally.

"What did you wish for?" Mother asked her.

"I was wishing to be fifteen, so I can wear nail polish."

"You don't have to waste a wish on that," smiled Father. "You'll get there."

"Why do they all want to be older?" Mother exclaimed, laying down her fork. "Time goes so fast anyway!" Four pairs of eyes turned on her, in wonder that she could ask such a question.

Father was filling his after-dinner pipe. He looked across the table at Mother. "I remember," he said, pointing his pipe stem at her, "when a certain young lady couldn't wait to be seventeen, so she could wear a formal evening gown at the Purim Ball. I know, because I took you to that ball."

Mother smiled, nodding her head.

"What color was the gown?" Sally put in eagerly.

"Pink," said Father, "with a kind of"—he waved the fingers of his right hand—"a kind of glitter in it."

"It had silver threads woven in," said Mother.

Sally's blue eyes were full of dreams. "How lovely!" she sighed. "I can just see it."

"Pop," said Joel, "was Mother as pretty then as she is now?" Again Mother stopped eating. She put a hand over her eyes and began to laugh.

"No," said Father, looking at her thoughtfully, "she wasn't. She was a bit too thin. And she didn't have that extra dimple in the left cheek."

"Oh, Dan! How can you be—" Mother couldn't go on, she was shaking so with laughter. Her cheeks were very pink, and the "extra dimple" showed up plainly.

They teased her about it until Alex suddenly exclaimed, looking down at his plate: "Something's happened to my birthday cake!"

"You ate it," said Sally. "I saw you."

Alex heaved a great sigh.

"I think we can do something about that," said Mother as she wiped her eyes.

All four children had another piece of cake.

"Now!" said Phil, getting up to open the presents.

"I vote that we begin with Joel's this time," said Alex.

"No!" shouted Joel. "You'll spoil the expense."

"*Sus*pense," said Father. While they laughed at Joel's mistake, Father put his hand consolingly on Joel's shoulder and patted the back of his neck. "How do *you* want it, Phil?"

"I want the suspense," said Phil. He opened Father's package first. It contained a wallet with a dollar bill inside.

Mother's present was a pair of Argyll socks she had knit herself.

"But I never saw you working on them," Phil said as he kissed her.

"You very nearly did," said Mother. "You remember that night you came down, after eleven, to have a new Band-Aid put on your thumb? Well, I pushed my knitting onto a chair behind the kitchen table just in time. And Father sat on it, to hide it."

Philip grinned widely. "Yes, I remember. That was a near thing."

"And all that your mother worried about," Father stated mournfully, "was whether she had dropped any stitches, not if the needles had stuck me!"

When he could do so, for laughing, Phil took up Alex's gift. It was a book about the stars, with charts and illustrations.

Philip and Alex shook hands. Joel could see they

were thinking of the good times they would have sharing the book. How he wished they would count him in!

Sally's tie was a very dark green, with little horse-shoes in old gold. There was a card with a wish on it:

Health to wear it,
Strength to tear it,
And money to buy another one!

Phil pulled off the tie he was wearing and put on the new one.

"Last, but not least," he said, and took the wrapping off Joel's present. Joel held his breath.

"Sure enough!" said Alex. "There's the sky-blue, the pink and the flowers all over."

Philip looked down at Joel, then back at the puzzle. I'll sure have a job putting this one together." He pulled Joel close to him and hugged him. "What a swell idea! I'm crazy about puzzles."

"I know," said Joel.

"You'll have to time me working out this one," said Phil to Alex.

"And I'm next with it," Alex said.

"Me next," came from Sally.

"I'd like to tackle it myself," said Father, "some evening when I have time."

"Time!" said Mother suddenly, and looked at the clock. "Past nine, Joel. School tomorrow."

The party was over, But as Joel brushed his teeth and washed his face and hands, getting ready for bed as slowly as possible, he knew he had done quite well that evening. He had only to keep on trying, and he would grow up too!

CHAPTER TWO

THE HANUKKAH LIGHTER

Five or six weeks had gone by since the jolly evening of Phil's birthday, and Joel was still doing well. His marks in school were good. The scooter-wagon helped him with his errands. The jigsaw puzzle was lots of fun, when someone in the family tried to put it together.

In fact, it wasn't until Hanukkah drew near that Joel was reminded he was the youngest in the family. It was queer, too, that Hanukkah should give him the helpless feeling he disliked so much, for Hanukkah was his favorite Jewish holiday of the whole year.

To begin with, it had such a wonderful story! Father had told him how a Greek king who ruled over the Land of Israel, long ago, had tried to make the Jewish people bow down and pray to the marble images of his own gods. But they believed in the one great God who made heaven and earth and everything in it. They wouldn't obey the cruel king, who sent his soldiers to kill them. But the Jewish people were fighting for their freedom, and they had a brave and clever general named Judah the Maccabee. So, little by little, they defeated armies that had three times . . . six times . . . ten times as many men as they had; and the Jews won back their country, and their capital city of Jerusalem and their beautiful white Temple.

They had to throw out the Greek idols of stone and marble, and purify the Temple before it was ready again for the worship of the one God. And when it came to rekindling the lights in the Menorah, the great golden lamp-holder tall as a man, they could find only one little jar of pure oil fit for use. It would last only twenty-four hours. But they lighted the lamps of the Menorah, and re-dedicated the Temple—made it holy again—with songs and music and thanksgiving to God. That's what the name Hanukkah meant. It was the Feast of Dedication. And, by a miracle, the lights that should have gone out in twenty-four hours burned for eight days and nights, until new oil could be purified! That is why Hanukkah is also called the Feast of Lights.

Joel always felt proud and happy, no matter how many times he heard the story. Even to think about it thrilled him.

Then why did he feel upset, now, because Sally, Phil and Alex were to act in the Hanukkah play at

Hebrew School? Joel knew he was always invited to their entertainments. Last year he had enjoyed watching them. He had clapped his hands for them and been proud of them. But this year it was different. He was eight years old. He wanted to take part in the holiday, not just sit still. He was jealous of the older ones.

"I don't see why I can't go to Hebrew School!" he complained to Mother that Thursday. The older ones had eaten their after-school snack and hurried away. Joel was still dawdling over a peanut-butter sandwich and his glass of milk.

"I've told you why, Joel," said Mother. "Father and I think it's better for you to play and be out of doors as much as possible. When you're ten it will be time enough for Hebrew School."

He gulped down the rest of his milk. Mother gave him an apple. "But Benjy Miller goes," Joel grumbled. "He's eight, like me."

"Maybe Benjy's parents don't have time to teach him the beginnings of Jewish history and religion. Father and I think it's better to start you ourselves."

Joel knew that answer too. He couldn't find anything wrong with it. But, just the same, he would have given a lot to be ten and to take part in the Hanukkah play. As he bit into his apple and ate it slowly, he thought that just to walk on the stage with a banner, or hold a sword and shout for Judah the Maccabee, would be the most wonderful thing he could wish for!

Sunday, things were no better. Sally, Phil and Alex stayed after lessons at Hebrew School, rehearsing the play; so dinner was later than usual. During the meal they talked about nothing else. Sally described the costume she was to wear. Phil teased her about it. Alex tried to speak in the deep voice of an old man. Joel could only listen and envy them. They had left him far behind.

He didn't ask for another piece of plum pie. When Mother offered it, he shook his head. "No, thank you, Mom," he said sadly.

She felt his forehead. "You're not feverish," she whispered. "What's the matter?"

Joel was glad to escape from the table. The older ones were too busy to notice him.

That afternoon Father, who was a high-school teacher, helped Alex study his lines. Alex, as one of the oldest students, had an important part in the play. With white hair and a white beard he was to be the old priest Mattathias, who, backed by his five tall sons—Judah among them—had started the revolt against the Greek king. Father also helped Phil, who was to be the Greek king's general.

In the living room Mother played the piano while Sally and four of her schoolmates rehearsed "The Dance of the Village Maidens," and their

part of "The Dance before the Temple" in the last act.

Joel went out to play, but found nobody to play with. His friend Harry Smith was busy wrapping the presents he was giving for Christmas, which, this year, would come soon after Hanukkah.

His friend Benjy Miller was learning a Hanukkah poem. He would recite it just before the play. Benjy asked Joel to hold the paper while he said the poem, to see if he knew it. Five times Benjy tried it, and still wasn't sure of the lines. By that time Joel knew the poem from beginning to end.

He went back home. Everyone was still busy.

He threw himself into a big armchair in the dining room and looked at the Hanukkah candlestick on top of the sideboard, where it waited nearly all the year for Hanukkah. It was made of brass, with eight arms that stood out—four on each side—like the branches of a tree. Each arm ended in a little cup to hold a candle; and there was another socket in the middle for a ninth candle, called the Shammos, or "servant of the lights," from which the other candles were lighted.

Joel remembered how the family had welcomed Hanukkah last year, when he was seven. On the first evening Father struck a match, lighted the Shammos and set it in the middle socket. Then Alex, as the eldest, chose the first candle out of the box and set it up in the first branch of the Menorah. Father handed him the Shammos, and he lighted the first candle while Father chanted the special blessing; and they all sang the Hanukkah hymn. That was all for the first night. But Hanukkah lasts for eight days and nights; and each evening one more candle is added, in memory of the miracle. So Alex and Phil both lighted candles on the second night; Alex, Phil and Sally on the third. Joel's chance didn't come until the fourth night. Last year he hadn't minded waiting his turn. But now he did mind, because he was a whole year older and felt he should have a greater share in the ceremonies.

The picture of Grandma, hanging against the

wall, gave him a new idea! He took down the Menorah. Grandma Mendoza, when she was alive, had always given it a good cleaning before the holiday, so that it gleamed as it reflected the light of the candles. He would clean it himself, this minute!

He put it on the kitchen table and brought out metal polish and soft rags. Now he was happy! He coated it all over with paste out of the can and was rubbing the base to a beautiful shine when the sounds of music and dancing ended in the living room. The rehearsal was over. Mother came in, followed by Sally.

"Joel, whatever are you doing?" Mother asked.

"Look at the mess!" cried Sally. "All over the new plastic tablecloth."

"Mom," he explained eagerly, "I'm cleaning the Menorah the way Grandma used to clean it."

"You're a sweet boy." Mother kissed him as she took away the rags and polish.

"But I want to do something for Hanukkah!" he almost shouted.

"I know you didn't mean to make a mess." She hugged him and patted him. "I'll help you with the polishing."

"I don't want to be helped!" he exclaimed. "I want to do it myself!" His face burned and his hair prickled, for Sally and her schoolmates were laughing at him. "Isn't he cute?" they said to one another.

Joel dashed down the hall. As he burst out of the apartment he could hear them telling Phil and Alex about it.

He ran all the way to Aunt Millie.

Aunt Millie, unlike most other grownups, was never too busy to understand what you said to her. For instance, she could be trusted to butter your bread. She didn't just slap a dab of butter on the middle of a slice, leaving the crusts bare, then ask: "Why don't you eat up all your bread? It's a shame to waste it, when so many children in the world are hungry!" Aunt Millie buttered it down to the edges, so you could eat it, crusts and all.

As it happened, she had company that Sunday afternoon; but she said to the gentleman "Excuse me," and took Joel into another room. While he was talking to her he thought of a fine plan, all his own, that would make Sally and Phil and Alex take notice of him! "Aunt Millie!" he interrupted himself. "I know what I can do!"

"Yes? Tell me," she smiled. "Very good," she said when he had finished. Out of a closet she took a stack of religious school magazines, for Aunt Millie sometimes taught on Sunday. "I think you'll find some pictures here that you can use. And I'll tell Mother I want you after school, so you can work on it here."

"But how will I get the gold paper and the crayons?" Joel asked. "I don't have any money left."

33

"TEMPLE ISRAEL"

He thought sadly of the strawberry whipped-cream sundae on which he had spent his week's allowance.

Aunt Millie had an answer for that. "You'll be getting Hanukkah spending money, won't you?"

His eyes lit up. "Dad always gives us a nickel for each year, so I'll have forty cents," he exclaimed.

"Then you can pay me back," she said, "and what you're doing will be all your own."

Hanukkah was here! It was suppertime on the first evening. Joel ate his fill of the holiday pancakes sprinkled with cinnamon, sugar and chopped nuts. He looked across at Aunt Millie and Grandpa Mendoza, who had been invited. They smiled encouragingly at him.

But Joel looked down at his plate. He felt very nervous. Perhaps what he had done would look silly to his sister and brothers. What if Alex laughed at it? Suppose Mother scolded him for sticking Scotch tape to the living-room wall?

At last, supper was over. Father took the little box of colored Hanukkah candles and led the way to the living room. Aunt Millie came next, pushing Joel before her. She led him to one side, so they could watch what happened.

On a brass tray, on a small table against the wall, the Menorah spread its eight branches. That's the way it was, every year. But behind it, this year, was an interesting made-up picture.

Two rows of pointed cypress trees in dark-green crayon made a path to the beautiful Temple, cut from the middle pages of a magazine. Its roofs and spires shone golden, and a golden sun rose in the East. Tiny flowers in red, blue and yellow made the front border, and little wings, two by two, edged the picture at the sides.

"Why! Who did that?" exclaimed Father.

"Joel," said Aunt Millie.

They were so quiet Joel held his breath. He could hear his heart thumping. Then Father broke the silence. "It's a fine idea," he said.

"It's beautiful," said Mother, and she looked admiringly at Joel.

Joel, with his eyes cast down, stood shyly first on one foot, then on the other. He was waiting to hear what Sally and the boys would say.

Sally said nothing. She just smiled and hugged him.

"What d'you know?" said Phil, patting him on the head.

"The kid's smart!" said Alex.

Then there was silence again. Joel glanced up at them. They weren't even looking at him. Alex was shifting the candles in the box with his forefinger. Phil was watching Alex. Sally was looking at her fingernails and rubbing them against the palm of her hand. . . . It didn't matter what he did. He was still "the kid," and they paid no more attention to him. He was back where he had started.

Aunt Millie, standing behind him, put her hands on his shoulders and gave them an encouraging squeeze.

Then Father came to his rescue. His gray eyes shining so you could see how pleased he was, he held out the box of candles to Joel. "You light the Shammos this year, son!" he said.

Joel stepped forward. He felt a little better as he picked out a red candle. "Red is for courage," Father said. Joel set it in the middle socket. He struck a match and lighted it. Alex chose yellow for the first candle. "Yellow is for happiness," said Father. Joel handed the Shammos to his big brother, who kindled the yellow candle and returned the Shammos to Joel. Joel set the Shammos in its place.

"Blessed art Thou, O Lord our God, King of the Universe," Father chanted, "Who hast made us holy with His commandments and hast bidden us light the Hanukkah candles."

Then they sang the Hanukkah hymn:

"Strengthening Power that made us free,
I will praise and honor Thee!"

At first Joel couldn't sing. His throat felt hard and dry. But the golden roof of his Temple gleamed at him, as he listened to the lovely, joyful old melody, the thought rose in his mind: You have to keep on trying. The story of Hanukkah proves it.

He joined in the singing. He sang so loud that Sally covered her ears, and Phil and Alex made signs for "Calm down!" with their hands.

Grandpa and Aunt Millie had gone home, and Father sat by himself in the living room. Joel came in quietly. Climbing onto the broad arm of Father's chair, he said: "I want to ask you something, Pop."

"Go ahead," said Father. His eyes were still on his book, but Joel knew he was listening.

"Look," said Joel. "I like everyone in the family. I wouldn't like anybody to be different. But— *why* did I have to be the youngest?" Joel slipped an arm behind Father's neck, to balance himself.

Father laid aside the book and put his arm around Joel. "We don't know why, Joel. You just *are*. But what's so bad about being the youngest?"

"Well . . . You can't ride a bicycle. You have to go to bed earlier. You don't have so much spending money. And that's only some of it."

"But many people think it's the best spot in the family. They say that when you're the youngest you get your own way a lot. You even get spoiled. Everyone makes a fuss over you and pets you—"

"But that's just what I don't like!" Joel exclaimed.

"Supposing *you* weren't the youngest," Father went on. "Then someone else would have to be.

And why should you wish what *you* don't like on someone else? Would that be right?"

"I guess not," Joel gave in.

Father patted his shoulders as he slid down. "You're all right, son!" he said. "You'll get there. All in good time."

CHAPTER THREE

A VISIT FROM UNCLE HARRY

It was not a good winter. There wasn't enough ice on the pond in Central Park for anyone to go skating. There wasn't enough snow to make a fort or a snowman, or to go "belly-whopping" in Mount Morris Park.

Joel wasn't the only one to be disappointed. Harry Smith, whose nicest Christmas present had been a sled big enough for five boys to pile onto, hardly had a chance to get it wet. It looked like new when the time came to put it away for next year.

Joel was glad when Mother no longer had to call after him "Put on your rubbers!" In school the class was drawing daffodils and tulips, and learning a poem about Spring. He could go without his mackinaw, and play ball out of doors after supper.

It seemed to fit in with this feeling of newness

and change, when Uncle Harry came to see them. Joel had noticed that after a visit from Uncle Harry something happened that was exciting or different.

He was not an ordinary uncle. He was Dr. H. Salo Mendoza, who worked for the World Health Organization of the United Nations. Because of some new discoveries he had made, his picture and his name had been in the newspapers.

Uncle Harry looked like Father—except that he wore a black mustache, while Father was clean-shaven; and where Father was just a tall man, Uncle Harry was long and thin as a ladder. Even Sally—two inches taller than Joel—said, laughing: "He makes you feel awfully small when he looks down at you from 'way up near the ceiling!"

Father and Uncle Harry had a private chat in the living room. Then Mother set the dining-room table with chocolate cake and fruit, and the grown-ups remained talking together for a long time. Before he went away, however, Uncle Harry wanted to see the children. Long past Joel's bed-time, he and Sally and the older boys sat around the table finishing the cake, along with cups of cocoa, and helping themselves politely when Mother passed them the box of candy Uncle Harry had brought.

Joel liked listening to the talk of the grownups. Even if some of the words they used were strange to him and he lost track of what they were saying, it showed him how many things there were for people to be interested in. It was like seeing pictures in a book that was still too hard to read. You promised yourself that someday you'd be able to enjoy it.

But there was something else that Joel noticed this evening. Though he had known it before, now it became important to him that Uncle Harry was Father's big brother; yet he didn't look down on Father. Once he asked Father's advice and, when it was given him, he said: "I think you're right, Dan. I hadn't thought of it that way."

Did it mean that a difference in age wouldn't matter so much, once you were older?

Joel felt that he *must* find out. After cleaning his teeth, getting into his pajamas, and being tucked in, he rose again, opened the bedroom door a crack and watched for Father to put out the lights.

"Tell me something, Dad!" he whispered.

"You still up?" Father gave him a mild spank. "Get to bed." But Joel could see that Father himself was excited about something.

"Pop," Joel asked, "how much older is Uncle Harry than you?"

"Three years," Father replied, puffing on his last pipeful.

"Then, when you were ten, he was thirteen?" That was the difference between Sally's age and Alex's.

Father nodded. Joel took a deep breath. "And when you were eight," he went on slowly and cautiously, "Uncle Harry was eleven?" That was Joel's own age as compared with Phil's.

"Correct," said Father.

"Thanks, Pop!" Joel exclaimed. He skipped off to bed.

Then it was true! The three years that made such an endless gap between himself and Philip— or between Sally and Alex—would make hardly any difference in time to come. He had seen the proof with his own eyes. Uncle Harry and his younger brother were equals and friends. Now Joel knew that it was possible to catch up with the older ones. He made up his mind to do it.

Meanwhile Purim, the Feast of Esther, was coming. It was a jolly holiday, with an exciting story which Joel had heard from Mother and Father every year since he was four.

They had told him how, long ago, Haman, the wicked adviser of the King of Persia, plotted to destroy all the Persian Jews. He was so sure of his power that he cast lots, to pick out a day on which they were to be slaughtered. But Esther, the beautiful queen, saved their lives, and that day became a day of thanksgiving and gladness on which, every year, Purim—the old Persian word for "casting lots," a custom something like our tossing of a coin —is gaily remembered.

Joel looked forward to this holiday, for Purim had always been fun.

To begin with, there was the Purim play—in which Sally, Phil and Alex were acting—at the Hebrew School. On the Sunday before Purim, Joel went with Mother and Father to see it. Sally was the favorite maid of Queen Esther. Phil took the part of a Persian lord. Alex was Mordecai, Queen Esther's Uncle, who by his wisdom helped to bring about the happy ending.

The play was so exciting that Joel could hardly sit still. He wanted to be in it. He was jealous of everyone on the stage, just as he had been at Hanukkah.

On the afternoon before the holiday, Sally brought home the Purim mask she had made in Hebrew School. It was a handsome face with a curly black beard, black eyebrows and a jeweled crown. She gave it to Joel. She said: "You can pretend to be the Persian King, Ahasuerus." He thanked her politely. Somehow he didn't care for masks any more.

Joel and the family always spent Purim Eve with Mother's parents, Grandpa and Grandma Jacobs. It was good to see Grandma, with the dark eyes twinkling in her round, pleasant face. And Grandpa exclaimed: "Joel's growing faster than anyone else!"

Playfully he put his hands under Joel's arms,

pretending to swing him up, as in former days. But after one try he shook his head, saying: "Impossible. Joel's a young man already!"

They had a wonderful meal, with the special

dainties always served at Purim. There were *kreplakh*—three-corner patties filled with a tasty mixture of meat and hard-boiled eggs. Joel had two helpings with his chicken soup. And after the dinner of roast chicken they had tea with lemon, in glasses, and *hamantaschen*—"Haman's pockets" —three-cornered cakes stuffed with poppy seed boiled in honey, or with prunes, or with chopped figs and nuts. Joel liked these so well that he had one of each.

After supper they all went to synagogue. Grandpa had given Joel an extra-loud noisemaker the size of a small flag. Joel held it in his hand and, as the reading of the Scroll of Esther began, he listened for the word "Haman." Though he didn't understand the Hebrew, he could recognize the villain's name. Then, along with all the children in the synagogue, he rattled his noisemaker while the grownups stamped their feet. It was better than just hissing at the villain, and Joel enjoyed that part of the holiday.

As the children came out of the synagogue, two ladies of the congregation gave every girl and boy a little box of chocolates, in honor of Purim. Joel ate his candy on the way home; but, though it tasted good, it didn't make up for the way he was feeling. Why wasn't Purim as much fun as it used to be?

The loud, lively chatter of Sally and the older boys floated back to him. He was lagging behind them—walking all by himself, since Mother and Father were strolling at the slower pace of the grandparents. I guess it's my own fault, Joel thought. I don't like doing baby things. I want Phil and Alex to notice me and count me in on their kind of fun.

He was glad to forget about his disappointment when he heard, next day, what Mother and Father had to tell them. It was not altogether a surprise. They had long saved and planned for it. Now they had done it.

They had bought a house and were going to move nearer to the high school in Brooklyn where Father taught! This would spare him the long, tiring subway ride back and forth each day. Besides, it was a big enough house so Aunt Millie and Grandpa Mendoza could live with them. Grandpa had been lonely since Grandma's death. Though he worked most of the day in his printing shop, he still had too much time to himself.

"We don't quite have the money," said Mother, "but Uncle Harry is helping us, because it will be so good for Grandpa."

Then Joel had been right! As always, Uncle Harry's visit had brought about a change. This one was as exciting as a gorgeous firecracker.

Sally hugged Mother and Father. "I wish Uncle Harry was here," she cried, "so I could hug him too!" She turned and made for Joel instead; but he backed away so quickly that everybody laughed, including Sally.

Alex stood silent, his face bright with joy. Joel

knew he had always hoped he would attend Father's high school when he was ready. Now he would have his wish. Suddenly his forehead wrinkled. "But I won't graduate!" he cried in alarm. "If I change schools in the middle of the term, they're sure to set me back!"

"You'll graduate!" said Father, waving his hand with the pipe in it. "You'll graduate in June, as planned. Only *you'll* do the subway riding, instead of your old Dad."

"Thanks, Pa! You think of everything," Alex sighed with relief.

It was Philip's turn to be unhappy. "Can't I go to the old school too?" he begged.

"We can't afford the extra carfare," said Mother firmly.

"Buck up!" Alex slapped him on the back. "It's only till June."

Joel, wide-eyed at the thought of moving, said nothing; but each day he finished his homework as quickly as possible, so he could help Mother with the packing. A good idea had come to him. This was his chance to get rid of those toys which Mother kept in memory of his babyhood, and which she brought out to show people just when he wanted them to forget he had been a baby.

He waited for the right moment. As Mother took the gaily painted duck and the sailor doll out of their special drawer, he said what he had often heard her say about other things: "Why keep these stuck away? Some child would enjoy them. Better give them to a little kid around here."

Mother shook her head. "Oh no," she laughed softly. "I couldn't bear to." She patted the toys, wrapped them in plenty of tissue paper and laid them carefully in the tray of a trunk. "You loved them so much! Why, you wouldn't go to sleep without Jack, here. They always remind me of you when you were a tiny little tad, so cute!" She closed the lid of the trunk and got up to bring the key. "No matter how tall you grow, you'll always be my baby!"

Joel was horrified. Of course he knew that nothing could stop him from growing, but he was shocked that she wanted to think of him always as a baby. More than ever, he felt he must get rid of those toys.

Mother was kneeling before the trunk, key in hand. Then, luckily for Joel, she was called to the telephone.

This was his chance. Pushing back the heavy lid, he snatched up the toys and softly closed the trunk again. He stole out to the street and ran around the corner.

He tore the tissue paper from the toys. He would break them into little bits, now and for always, so he would never be bothered with them again. Angrily he jerked at the string by which he used

49

to pull the duck. Donald Duck quacked appealingly. Jack, the sailor-boy, never stopped smiling. Joel hadn't the heart to smash them. Why not give them to a child? But there was no one in the street.

As he wandered around the block, Joel noticed Mr. Hendricks, the janitor of a neighboring apartment house, standing near his cellar door. Joel went up to him. "We're moving," he said eagerly, "and we've got no room for these. Would your little boy want them?"

"Why, yes! Thank you." Mr. Hendricks took the toys carefully in his big hands. "Willis would like these very much." Then he looked at Jack and at Donald Duck again. "But they're very nice. Not a bit broken. Sure your mother doesn't want them?"

"Oh, they're mine!" Joel called out over his shoulder. "I can do what I like with them."

"Thank you—very—much!" said Mr. Hendricks.

Joel looked back before he turned the corner. Mr. Hendricks was carrying them indoors.

CHAPTER FOUR

JOEL AT THE SEDER

Mother forgot she hadn't locked the trunk in which she had so carefully packed Joel's baby playthings. When she came back after the telephone call, she began to put sweaters into a suitcase and paid no more attention to the trunk.

In the new house, as Mother hunted through the pile, and her long, clever fingers quickly folded, sorted, or laid aside what she found, there was a worried look on her face. "Oh dear!" she sighed. "I wouldn't have lost those toys for the world!"

Joel couldn't feel sorry for what he had done. But he was sorry for Mother and didn't want her to be upset. So he told himself that he would make up for it by helping her, and by making her glad he was a big boy now and not the silly "little tad" she remembered.

They had moved on a Wednesday, because that happened to be the last day of the month. Early Thursday morning Alex set out for the subway station, since he was to ride to the old school. Mother went with Phil and Sally, who were taking their transfer cards to the new school.

But Joel said calmly: "Why don't I stay home and help you, Ma? Time enough to begin school on Monday. I know my writing and I've read *Our Community* all through, twice. I can't miss much."

Mother looked pleased, though thoughtful. Her brown eyes studied Joel. She liked to have him with her. "If you'll really help," she said, "and not just get in my way."

Joel really helped. While she was away at the school, he washed and dried the breakfast dishes. When she returned, he plumped up pillows and helped her spread sheets and covers on the beds. He cut lengths of paper, plain or fancy, for lining drawers and shelves while she unpacked and hung clothes in the closets and put away linens and underwear in bureau drawers. He scrubbed potatoes and shelled peas. He went for milk and eggs and butter to a neighboring store, which was four blocks away.

Joel liked everything about the new house—especially the back garden, in which there were a magnolia tree with big, rosy buds and a huge oak tree down at the further end. Father had promised to hang a swing from a branch of the oak.

Joel liked the house because you could spread out in it, upstairs and down. There were banisters to slide on. He and Phil and Alex shared the large room on the third floor, with three windows each facing a different way.

On the second floor Grandpa Mendoza had the largest room, with the sun porch looking out on the back garden. He had books and pictures, his big

armchair and Grandma's rocking chair, a beautiful set of chessmen on a black table inlaid with mother-of-pearl, and so many other things that reminded him of happy times in his past that he needed a lot of space.

There was another large corner room for Father and Mother, and a third one, not quite so large, which Sally shared with Aunt Millie.

On Monday morning Mother went to the school with Joel. The principal, Mr. Adams, shook hands with her. He remembered seeing her on Thursday. He smiled and said: "Are you getting used to Brooklyn? I hope you'll like us!"

"I do already," said Mother.

Mr. Adams was glad to hear that Joel liked school and had always done well at his lessons. It was all very pleasant, until Mother left and Mr. Adams led him along the corridors and up the stairs to the new class. Then Joel felt as if cold air were blowing on him. For he dreaded the moment when he would have to face a classroom full of strange boys and girls, all staring at him. He told himself: "What are you afraid of? They can't eat you!" But the chilly feeling stayed with him until they entered the third-grade room. Then he suddenly became very warm. His cheeks burned and he blinked at the rows and rows of eyes.

He felt better when he looked at Miss Keegan, for she smiled at him. She had black hair and rather thick eyebrows and rosy cheeks. "Does it matter where I put you, Joel?" she asked in a friendly voice. "Can you see the blackboard from any part of the room?"

He shook his head at the first question but found his voice for the second. "Yes, ma'am," he said. "I can see all right."

She seated him next to a sandy-haired boy in the

middle of the room. Joel was glad when the lesson continued and the children forgot about him.

"How's the new teacher?" Father asked him that evening at supper.

"Miss Keegan's all right," he said. "I think I'll like her."

"Good!" said Mother. "It makes all the difference when you like your teacher."

"Sure does!" Sally exclaimed.

"But I—I hate going into a class where I don't know anyone!" Joel burst out.

Father chuckled. "It's like the first plunge into cold water, son. After a few minutes you warm up!"

But by the end of that week, although he answered properly, the few times Miss Keegan called on him, Joel still hadn't "warmed up," and not one of his classmates had spoken to him outside of school.

On the block where the house stood, it just happened that there wasn't a boy or girl his own age. He had no one to play with and he felt lonely.

There was a girl, Sylvia, in the house next door. She had blue eyes and long curls, and she was nearly as tall as Joel. But she was only six and her brother was just a baby.

Joel was very glad when Grandpa Mendoza and Aunt Millie moved in, early the second week. He helped them put away their belongings. It made breakfast a more interesting meal, seeing their bright, friendly faces above the cereal bowls. Grandpa Mendoza had a funny way of squinting his eyes at you, as if you were something worth looking at. The older children also noticed that little habit and felt flattered by it. They were happy to have Grandpa and Aunt Millie with them.

But Joel had an extra reason for welcoming Grandpa, a reason he kept to himself. Passover was coming. At the Seder supper with which the festival opens, it is the youngest child in the house who has a special part. Joel would be the one to ask the Four Questions, beginning with "Wherefore is this night different from all other nights?" And Father would read the answer, leading off with "Slaves were we unto Pharaoh in Egypt," out of the Haggadah—a picture book giving the story of the festival, the arrangement for the supper, and songs and legends that went with it.

Joel had always asked the questions in English, but this year he wanted to try something new—something that would make Sally, Phil and Alex notice and think well of him. Suppose he learned to ask the Four Questions in Hebrew? "That ought to put me on the map," he said to himself. He was going to surprise them.

Grandpa came home from his printing shop early, these days. He was happy to help Joel with the surprise. Every afternoon they worked for about half an hour, and Joel soon learned to recognize the squarish black letters of the Hebrew language. Presently he could read the words with expression.

Meanwhile, at school, the class was painting Easter eggs. Joel colored one violet and another yellow. Others he made green and blue and orange. When he brought them home, Mother put them in a dish of ferns on the supper table. They made a pretty centerpiece.

"It's funny," Joel remarked. "Other people have Easter eggs. And at the Seder, on Passover, we always have eggs too. I wonder why?"

"That's not hard to explain," said Father. "Easter and Passover are both spring festivals. That's the season when eggs are most plentiful. They've always meant young life, and the new beginning of Nature's year. So they've become a sign of gladness and promise."

The days passed slowly for Joel; then at last it was Passover.

He watched Aunt Millie spread Mother's best white tablecloth and arrange on it the special dishes, each of which had a meaning for tonight.

In the silver candlesticks used only to welcome the Sabbath and Jewish holidays, Mother lighted the candles. Spreading her hands above them, she recited the blessing; the holiday had begun.

They took their seats at the Seder table; and the Haggadahs were opened, in memory of that springtime, nearly thirty-five hundred years ago, when Moses led their people out of Egypt.

Joel had his own reason for feeling excited. He smiled at Grandpa, who nodded wisely at him as if to say: "We'll show them!"

Then Grandpa chanted the prayer which makes the Sabbath or festival holy, and sang in Hebrew the blessing on wine. It was part of the ceremony that the children's glasses, too, had been filled; and as Grandpa and the grownups drank, the youngsters also took a sip of the sweet red wine. Joel felt it warming his throat pleasantly as it went down.

Father began to read from the Haggadah—in English, so they could all understand. Soon the time came for Joel to ask the questions.

He drew in a quick breath and his heart hammered. What if he made a mistake and the others laughed at him?

Everyone was waiting. Father said kindly: "Go on, son. Don't be shy with *us!*" Grandpa smiled, looking very proud.

Joel found his voice and began to read. He read

the whole paragraph clearly and without an error. Glancing up for a moment while he read, he saw Father beaming at him. "In Hebrew!" Mother whispered to Aunt Millie. As he finished, Joel knew that he couldn't have done better.

"Joel! You're so smart!" cried Sally, throwing her arms around him. For once Joel didn't want to escape.

"Smart as they come," said Phil, smiling in his own funny way, one end of his mouth tighter than the other.

"He won't need Hebrew School!" Alex exclaimed, throwing up his hands. "He knows it all now!"

"No, I don't," said Joel, modest but delighted. "I only know this."

"Then *I'll* read the questions in English," said Sally; and she did so, very nicely.

Father began the answer. Joel listened, feeling warm and happy. Never had the Seder been so interesting to him. Here was the roasted bone that represented the Passover lamb eaten on the last night in Egypt. There on a covered plate in front of Father were the *matzoth,* the unleavened bread that made this holiday different from all others. They reminded you that, when the call came to leave Egypt and be free, the Hebrews couldn't wait for their bread to rise. They had taken up the dough —wrapping it, bowl and all, in clean cloths—and

61

carried it away on their backs. The hot sun baked it flat and hard as these *matzoth*.

Father broke one and recited the blessing on bread:

"Blessed art Thou, O Lord our God,
King of the Universe,
Who bringest forth bread from the earth."

Then followed the special blessing on *matzoth*. Joel took a bite of the hard crackerlike *matzoth* when Father handed him a piece. He knew he'd better not eat much of it, though he was hungry; for there were many good things coming.

Next he had a pinch of the *moror*, the grated horseradish that burned your tongue and reminded you of the bitterness and sorrow of slavery. He took a little more on the *matzoth*, which made it easier to eat. But Alex, who had boldly put a teaspoonful in his mouth, coughed while Phil pounded his back. When he could catch his breath Alex only laughed, though the tears came to his eyes.

"Now for *haroseth*!" Sally said happily. This was the delicious paste, made of apples, nuts, prunes, and wine, which stood for the sweetness of freedom. It was so good that Mother had to remind them: "Not too much, children! Leave some space for supper."

Then came the hard-boiled eggs, which represented the sacrifices that used to be offered in the Temple at Jerusalem. Joel ate one, dipping it in salt water to remind himself of the tears shed in slavery.

Now supper was served. Joel ate chicken broth with *matzoth* balls, roast chicken, and a helping of *matzoth* pudding made with fruit and almonds. It was all delicious.

With his last spoonful of pudding, however, he became a little drowsy. He sat up with a start. On this one night, when he was allowed, even encouraged, to stay up along with the older ones, it would never do to give in. That would really show him up as a baby. Other years he had never quite managed to last it out, and had fallen asleep in his chair. This year— never!

Near Father's end of the table stood a tall glass brimming with wine. Nobody had drunk from it. For this was the special glass for the Prophet Elijah. Father had told Joel many stories about Elijah, who had been carried up to heaven in a chariot of fire and who sometimes came to earth again to help poor, suffering folks in their time of greatest need. Especially at Passover he might come to help his people celebrate the Season of Our Freedom, as the festival was called.

So, when the Seder began again, Joel decided he must stay awake to watch for the Prophet. Presently Alex went to let him in. He opened the dining-room door and the front door, so that Elijah might enter. As Alex returned and sat down again, Joel watched with awe. His eyes opened wide. Perhaps, just tonight, Elijah might come! Maybe—maybe . . . Who could tell?

Alex went to close the doors again. The Prophet —if he were coming—must be here. Perhaps he would drink from his glass. Joel's eyes returned every few moments to the tall goblet. The wine never seemed to go any lower. Not yet. But if that wonder *should* happen, Joel was going to be the first one to notice it!

He didn't fall asleep, though his eyes were smarting. The Seder came to an end. Mother and Aunt Millie were leading the family in the songs with which, by old custom, the evening was happily completed. Joel sang with them "God of Might, God of Right." Then came long tuneful chants of which only the grownups knew all the words. Finally they began the best of all—the "house-that-Jack-built" song about "One Only Kid." It told about the many narrow escapes of the baby goat that represents Israel, and how, with God's help, it came safely through all dangers and is still alive.

Smiling around him and blinking with tired eyes, Joel heartily joined in the refrain: "One Only Kid! One Only Kid!"

It was over. For the first time in his life Joel had

remained awake for the whole evening of the Seder. Father slapped him on the back. "Good for you, old scout!" Sally, Phil and Alex raised a cheer.

Joel had never been so happy in his life.

For the first two days of the holiday, while they stayed home from school, Joel had the delightful feeling that his brothers and sister were very pleased with him and included him in whatever they did.

Then school began again, and they seemed to move further and further ahead of him. Again he was left behind.

For instance, Sally, Phil and Alex went to see a movie. When she came home, Joel asked Sally to tell him about it. Now, Sally loved to talk about movies; for she wanted to be an actress someday. That, or a famous dress designer for movie stars. But this time she said to Joel: "The picture was too old for you. You wouldn't be interested."

Another time, when they were having their after-school snack, Sally was complaining of her arithmetic homework. "Decimals are a pest!" she said.

"Oh, they're not bad," remarked Phil. "I'll show you!"

"What's *decimals*?" asked Joel.

"You'll know when you get there," said Phil. "You're not up to it yet."

Worse still was the setback Joel had that evening when he joined the three older ones in the dining room. They were talking excitedly about the end of the world, and the things that might cause it.

"Sh-h!" said Alex when he noticed Joel. Silence fell. Then Alex asked Joel kindly: "Don't you have any pals yet?"

Joel shook his head.

"That's a shame," said Phil. "How come?"

"I guess he's shy," Sally said gently. "But you're sure to make friends at school," she added.

"I guess so." After a moment Joel went away. No sooner was the door closed than the chatter of their voices rose again. It made Joel feel small. At the same time he couldn't find anything wrong with their behavior, for he knew they meant it kindly. They didn't want to scare him.

He went into the kitchen, where Mother was knitting while she listened to music on the radio. "What a long face, Joel!" she said pleasantly, and turned the music very low. "What's the matter?"

He told her how he felt because the others wouldn't let him in on their talk.

"I'm afraid that can't be helped, dear," Mother said. "As you learn more and have wider interests, and there are more things you can talk about, they'll just naturally count you in."

Joel still looked unhappy.

"Right now," she continued, "it's as if you didn't speak the same language. Suppose we were traveling somewhere—in France, let's say—and we were strangers. I might like you and want to talk to you. I might say in French: 'Who's this nice boy?' But if you didn't know French, you wouldn't understand I was paying you a compliment."

He nodded slowly.

"It isn't that they don't like you," said Mother. "You know that."

Joel thanked Mother, and she kissed him. Her explanation did make him feel better, as though he'd taken medicine. But he knew, now, he must keep on trying. He was still 'way behind.

CHAPTER FIVE

A DIRTY FACE AND A
NEW ADMIRER

When Aunt Millie came home from work, if she had nothing special to do and if she didn't expect company that evening, she would read aloud to Joel. She was reading *Tom Sawyer* and they usually went into Grandpa's room, or out onto his porch if it was warm enough. Grandpa enjoyed listening, for he had not read the book since he was a boy no older than Joel.

One night after supper Joe was helping in the kitchen. He wiped the table silver and polished it with a soft cloth, wondering meanwhile what would happen to Tom and his girl friend Becky. They hadn't realized they were wandering away from the grown-up sight-seers and were now lost in the endless cave.

"Isn't it exciting?" he exclaimed to Aunt Millie. Then, to Mother: "Remember where Tom and

Becky see a light, and they hope it's someone coming to find them? But, when the man comes, it's Injun Joe, who would kill Tom if he saw him. Imagine being lost and having to hide from Injun Joe too!"

Mother closed the refrigerator. Walking past him, she touched his chin and remarked: "Your face is dirty."

"But I washed my hands and face before supper!" he exclaimed.

"Look in the glass," said Mother calmly.

Kneeling on his chair so he could see into the little mirror beside the kitchen door, he saw it was true. There was a brownish smear on his cheek and chin. He wet the corner of a paper towel from the kitchen roll and scrubbed his face.

"That's better," said Mother.

But Joel felt as flat as a balloon when the air goes out of it. He didn't want to talk about the book any more. What did a little bit of dirt matter? Yet Mother had let such a common, everyday thing as a smudge on his face break up the wonderful remembrance of *Tom Sawyer*.

He slipped out the back door as soon as possible. At the foot of the porch steps, where the garden path began, he stood quite still, puzzling about the way grownups always notice a little dirt on you before they pay attention to anything else. After all he wasn't a kid playing with mud pies. He never knew where the dirt came from. Why fuss about it, anyway?

In the garden next door, Sylvia was riding her tricycle. She pedaled at a great rate, making the most of the last precious minutes before bedtime.

Suddenly, as she passed along the wall of her house that was nearest to Joel, she jerked aside with a terrified scream. She jumped from her tricycle and started to run.

"What are you scared of, Silly?" Joel called out, straightening the tricycle which had tipped over sideways. "It's only me!"

Sylvia stopped and turned to look. "Who-o-o?" she stammered in her fear.

"I'm Joel, from next door. Who did you think I was?"

She came back slowly, her teeth chattering. "A—a—a ghost," she said.

"Come back here," Joel said. "You can pinch me; then you'll know I'm real."

He bent his arm and she clutched it above the elbow. He could tell that she was still afraid, for she was trembling. He made her sit on the porch steps next to him.

"Where did you get that nonsense about ghosts?" he asked. "Did you ever see a ghost?"

She shook her head, but after a while she whispered: "It comes in the dark. It jumps on you."

"Who told you that?"

"Stewy."

"Stewy!" He said angrily. That was Stewart Bleeker, the tall boy who lived on the other side of her house. Joel had noticed him among the older boys. He had a mop of straw-colored hair and a spiteful grin.

"He's big," she said in little gasps. "Much bigger than you. He knows all about them." She looked at the dark branches waving against the deep-blue sky. In the light of the curving silver moon the shadows seemed to leap forward, then dodge away. She shivered.

Joel was sorry for her. He remembered how terrible it felt when, long ago, he had been afraid of the dark. Besides, she was only a girl.

"Don't let him scare you. My Dad says there aren't any ghosts, and he's much bigger than Stewy. And he knows much more. My Dad's a teacher in high school, and he knows—" Joel spread out his arms, to show there was no measuring Father's knowledge.

"Yes?" Sylvia looked up hopefully.

"It's something people invented ages ago, just to scare themselves with," Joel said grandly. "None of that stuff is real. My father says so."

On her forehead the worried wrinkle seemed to smooth itself out. She smiled and sat up straight. "You're awful smart, Joel," she said gratefully. "I won't listen to Stewy any more."

71

"That's it. Don't give him the satisfaction," Joel said. "When I'm bigger I'm going to fight him for scaring you!"

She laughed so that her dimples showed. The fear was all gone now and she looked quite comfortable with her elbows resting on her knees and her face between her hands. "I won't be such a baby any more!" she promised.

"Sylvia!" her mother called. "Come in. Bedtime!"

"Don't you hate that?" She got up slowly.

"I don't have to go for another hour," he said, very pleased to be eight.

"Guess I'll have to. So long!" she said. But she kept turning to look back at him, and she waved before the door closed behind her.

After that, in the evening, Sylvia made long pauses when her tricycle reached the side of the house nearest to Joel's. If he came out she seemed very happy and listened to everything he said. Joel guessed that she thought more of him than any other boy she knew. He said to himself: "She's only a kid!" Nobody he could play with.

But he got tired of playing "catch" by himself, and "flipping" pictures of baseball players by himself. Sylvia was always nearby, watching him. Presently he showed her how to throw a ball properly. She didn't do well at that, but she made a good pioneer woman when they played at going

72

out West in a covered wagon. He got out the tricycle he hadn't ridden for a long while; and they played at bicycle racing, with Joel giving her a good, long start.

This wasn't what he wanted. He wished that his old friends Harry Smith and Benjy Miller lived here. It was no fun walking home from school alone, kicking a pebble ahead of him. There had to be someone to scuffle with, someone to get the pebble away. Then Joel could try to get it back again from his playmates. . . .

Sally and Philip had found themselves companions among their classmates. But Joel still felt too "new" and shy to start a friendship, though he had been at this school almost a month.

One afternoon, when he was doing his homework in the living room and Mother was sewing near the window, he said suddenly: "Why am I so shy, Mom?"

"Why *are* you?" Mother laughed a little. "I don't know why you should be. Mostly, people are shy when they think they're not so good as others. They think other people are smarter, or better looking, or better dressed, or better liked. But you don't have any such reasons for feeling shy or being afraid to open your mouth among strangers." Mother put aside her sewing and sat down beside him at the table. She stroked his forehead, brushing back the hair. "What's the matter?"

"Nothing," he said. "Only—Miss Keegan sent me to the fourth-grade teacher with a note, and I felt awful. Everyone in the classroom stared at me." His face felt hot at the memory of it.

"But that was a compliment, to be picked as teacher's messenger."

"I know," he said, "but I'm shy. I don't know how to start a conversation with the other boys in school, so I've got no one to play with. I don't know how to *stop* being shy." He felt ashamed that he was so different from his brothers and Sally.

"I'll tell you how," said Mother readily. "When you meet someone new, you just think about what the other person might like you to do; then you'll forget to be shy. Perhaps the other child is shy too. How do you know?"

Joel brightened up. "I'd like to try it, Mom," he said. "I'd like to try right away. But—but what could I do?" He looked at her eagerly, ready for anything.

Mother thought awhile. Then she suggested: "Why don't you go to some of the other mothers on the block, just as you came to me this afternoon, and ask them, too, if they'd like to order plants for Arbor Day?"

"Swell!" Joel bounced up. "Thanks, Mom!" He put his pencil in the sharpener on Father's desk, gave it a nice sharp point, took his notebook and went out.

74

He started with the house on the other side of Sylvia's. This was Stewy Bleeker's house. Joel opened the gate, walked up the garden path, went up the steps to the porch and rang the bell. As he heard footsteps in the hall, his heart began to hammer and his mouth felt dry.

A tall woman opened the door. She had light brown hair turning gray, and sharp eyes that reminded him of Stewy's mischievous ones. "What is it?" she asked.

Joel was tongue-tied. His mouth wouldn't open. His cheeks burned.

"Well, what do you want?" she asked. "I haven't got all day."

What Joel wanted very much was to be back in his own house! Then he remembered that Mother had told him to think of what the *other* person wanted. "Do you want some plants, ma'am?" he burst out. "Our school is ordering plants from a nursery, for Arbor Day, and you could have some, too, if you want them."

"Plants?" Mrs. Bleeker said. "What kind?"

"Here." Joel handed her his notebook, opened at the page that listed, in his neat printing:

IVY - 3c
BEGONIAS - 6c
GERANIUMS
PINK OR RED - 19c

She glanced up at Joel. "Why didn't my boy Stewart tell me about this?"

"Because he's a big boy. The older ones aren't doing this. They're going to plant a tree in the park, for Arbor Day."

"That's nice," said Mrs. Bleeker. "I'll take a begonia and a geranium."

"Red or pink?"

"Red, I guess."

"You have to pay for it now," said Joel, "then it will be all ready, with the flowers out, when I bring it to you."

"When will that be?"

"In about two weeks," said Joel.

She gave him a quarter and he began slowly to print her name on a new page. "Do you want me to write it?" she offered.

"Yes, please." He gladly handed her the book and pencil. She wrote:

Mrs. Bleeker, 1 beg. 1 ger. red 25¢

She smiled and nodded. "Thanks, young man!" she said briskly, and closed the door.

Joel hopped down off the porch and out of the gateway, he felt so set up. "Young man," Stewy's mother had called him. Mother was right. He needn't be shy!

At the house around the corner, on the avenue, a young woman wearing a checked apron and a dust cap gave him six cents and ordered a begonia.

At the next two houses he rang the bell and waited, but nobody was home.

Further down the block an old gentleman opened the door. He perched a pair of glasses on his nose and looked through them at Joel's list.

"Three cents?" He pointed to the ivy. "How can they make it so cheap?"

"The ivy's little," Joel answered. "But it will grow. They're all good. My teacher had some in school, to show us."

"What can I lose?" the old man chuckled. "Give me three." He added his name and address to Joel's orders in the notebook and gave him nine cents.

On the street running parallel to his own, Joel met with his first refusal. A nice-looking lady turned off the sprinkler on her lawn and met Joel halfway down the garden path. "No," she said, "I'm not taking any, thank you. I'm ordering some plants from my own little boy. But thanks for coming, anyway!"

"You're welcome," said Joel, and was turning away when a thought struck him. Joel spoke up: "Then he goes to my school. What grade is he in, ma'am?"

"The third grade," said the lady.

"Why, he must be in my class!"

"Then you must know him!" she smiled. She called out: "Leo! Here's one of your classmates."

A boy of Joel's age came running from the back

garden and stopped suddenly at sight of Joel. Sure enough, this was Leo Posner! He was grinning and twisting a little cowlick of dark hair, just as he did in class when he stood up to answer a question. The cowlick stood out like a small horn above his left eye. Does he do that because he's shy, Joel wondered.

"Hello," he said to Leo. "I didn't know you live so near me."

"Where do *you* live?" Leo came forward.

"Next street. Around the block."

"Well—hang around," said Leo. "I'll get my roller skates."

"I've got to finish this, first," said Joel eagerly. "But I'll come right back. I'll bring my skates."

Around the next corner a stout lady with red hair and dimples was standing at the garden gate. "Oh no! I've got to keep this in the family." While she was speaking, a girl with freckles on her small, sharp nose, and long dark braids wound around her head and tied with a ribbon, came out. Joel recognized her.

"Hello!" she said. "You're the new boy, aren't you?"

"Yep," said Joel, nodding.

"Come in," said Gracie Michaels, who was nine years old. She took his hand and brought him to her twin brother, Jerry.

Jerry was throwing a ball so that it hit the ground

a few inches in front of the house wall, bounced up against the wall, then flew back into his hands. He did it again and again, counting out loud: "Fifteen, sixteen, seventeen . . ."

"Jerry, here's—"

"Sh-h!" whispered Joel, knowing that Jerry didn't want to be interrupted.

"Eighteen, nineteen, twenty. There, I did it!" He straightened up and said "Hello" to Joel. His greenish-gray eyes and curly red hair made him look very different from his twin.

"You live around here?" Gracie asked.

"Next street," said Joel.

"We'll be seeing you, then," said Gracie. "Have you done your homework?"

"Sure," said Joel.

"How did you do that last example?" Gracie ran to the porch and brought him her exercise book.

"You can't answer that," said Joel. "You can't take a larger amount from a smaller one."

Jerry came nearer and stared down at the book. "But—why would she give us such a real hard example?"

"That's a catch. I guess Miss Keegan wants to see if we know our stuff."

"See? I told you," said Gracie to her brother. He shrugged. "Where are you going now?" she asked Joel.

"I have to go home, first. Then I told Leo Posner I'd bring my roller skates."

"We're coming too!" said Gracie. "Meet you at Leo's." Joel looked at Jerry. Jerry nodded.

Joel ran home for his skates. "Here, Mom! Take care of these for me!" he said happily, giving her his notebook and the money. "I'll tell you afterward—"

"Supper's at half-past six, Joel," said Mother. "Be back in time."

That afternoon Joel had more fun than at any other time since he had moved to the new neighborhood.

After that he came home from school with Leo every day; sometimes Jerry joined them. It wasn't a lonely trip any more.

Other things weren't going so well for him, however. The brown turtle-neck sweater that Phil had outgrown was now to be his. He was supposed to wear it on cool or rainy mornings. Phil hadn't liked it because once in a while it became itchy. Not every time, for in that case Mother wouldn't expect you to wear it. Only sometimes, and for no reason you could give, it scratched unbearably. Joel despised it.

Of course the clothes that he wouldn't mind wearing—those of Alex or Phil—never lasted long enough to get to him. The pullover with the reindeer across the chest and the Hopalong Cassidy shirt were worn through at the elbows and ripped down the back before the older boys outgrew them.

"That's another nuisance about being the youngest," Joel grumbled one evening when Mother was mending winter clothes before putting them away until fall. "You have to wear someone else's old clothes. I like my own clothes—the ones you buy for *me*."

"I know, Joel. It's too bad. But with the price that children's clothes are, these days, I'm only too glad we have a tailor in the family."

Joel kicked at a chair leg. This was another sore point. Uncle Si always sent Joel the clothes he had made for his son Marty, when Marty outgrew them. A box of these, cleaned, pressed and neatly repaired, had arrived by parcel post the day before.

"They're such *good* things!" Mother had exclaimed happily. Now she said: "We could never afford to buy such clothes for you."

"I hate them," said Joel. "They never have enough pockets."

"Boys like pockets, but tailors don't," Father remarked, "because the things you stuff into them get the clothes out of shape. But we know how you feel!" He sighed and shrugged his shoulders.

"*That* thing," said Joel, glaring at the navy blue mackinaw he would be wearing next winter. "Look at those sissy buttons!"

Mother looked. She had thought them very nice buttons. They were dark red with a slanting band of gold across them. Now she saw what Joel meant. "I'll change them," she said; and she did, for plain dark blue ones with navy anchors.

In the big room at the top of the house, Joel's things were being pushed into a corner. His cot was now between the door of the room and a low wall that joined the slope of the attic ceiling. His little bookcase was jammed behind the bed, so that only the upper shelves could be reached easily.

It didn't bother Joel; for there was always something interesting to watch in the room, while his brothers were in it.

For instance, in Phil's class at school they were making a puppet theater. Phil was chairman of the committee that was to build the stage and work the curtains. So he had to have room for the model stage he was making.

The fish tanks were placed on Joel's bureau. Joel didn't mind. He liked to be with the older boys when they watched the guppies and the golden sawtails and the black-and-gold "striped reds" in the tank of tropical fish. It was interesting to hear Alex dictate notes to Philip about them, and about the plants and shells under water.

Now Phil was sawing and planing wood to make a birdhouse for the back garden, because Alex was sure he had heard a brown thrasher singing in the oak tree. All this activity went on during week ends, and Joel was glad, for he had seen robins on the lawn, and was delighted to think that a robin family might grow up in the little house.

Sometimes the room became a laboratory with microscope and test tubes and the chemistry set Alex had been given when he was twelve. Smells and flashes made the very air exciting to Joel; and there were slides at which he was invited to look, showing the wonderful cells that made up the skin, or what potato peel really looked like, or onion parings or scraps of cheese—all turned to magic by the microscope.

Other days, from an easel made by Phil, they hung a chart showing the human figure, with all parts of the body labeled so you could see the liver

and the lungs and heart and stomach. What fascinated Joel particularly was a big black-and-white drawing of a skeleton, copied by Alex from the encyclopedia downstairs.

On rainy afternoons Alex would lie flat on his stomach reading aloud to Phil, who sat on the next cot, listening and asking questions, his arms wrapped around his knees. Joel listened, too, when he could understand the reading. He even asked questions, which were carefully answered.

Since Joel was the one being crowded, and since he didn't mind, it was a shock to him when he heard his brothers complain. Alex said to Father, one afternoon, that he and Philip hadn't enough space for the things they wanted to do.

Phil said: "After all, it's an attic room. The ceiling's low in places." Then he looked straight at Joel and said: "Three's too many up there."

"Why? What did I do?" cried Joel.

Philip said, not answering Joel but speaking directly to Father: "He never puts anything away!"

His brown eyes wide and hurt at such an injustice, Joel turned to Father. "They can talk!" he protested. "Their slides, and their fish food, and their boxing gloves, and their test tubes, and their books—they're all over everything! Come up and see!"

"The room's a mess," said Father. "I've heard about it from Mother and Sally. But naturally"—

85

he turned to Joel—"Alex and Phil think *their* junk is all right!"

"I think it's all right too!" Joel said quickly to his brothers. "I never said anything, did I? I like to see what you're doing. Why do you want to put me out?"

"You can come up whenever you like," Alex assured him, sorry that Joel was hurt. He put his hand on the younger boy's shoulder and said: "We're not going to charge you admission!"

Joel felt as if he were in an elevator, going down very fast. There was no dodging the fact: his big brothers didn't want him in their room.

CHAPTER SIX

A STEP UP

"But how can you feel crowded in that great big room?" said Mother when Alex and Phil took their complaint to her. "It's the whole top of the house. Why, it's big enough for six boys!"

"For their bodies, yes," remarked Father. "But I've noticed that the spirit always takes up more room than the body."

"Then what shall we do?" Mother was seated in her rocking chair—rocking rather fast, as she did when something worried her.

Father put the papers he had been marking into his brief case and locked it, before he answered: "I have only one suggestion, dear. But I know what you've been planning, and it seems a shame to—"

"I suppose you mean my linen room," she sighed. Joel knew she was thinking of the little extra room between the corner bedroom and the bathroom. "I did hope that, when school closed, you'd make me some shelves for it."

"I still can," said Father quietly. "There's nothing wrong with that. You certainly have a right to something you want."

"But if the boys feel so cramped," she murmured, "it would be a shame to use a room just for storing sheets and towels."

"If you feel that way," Father said, "then why not let one of the boys have it. But it's for you to say, my dear."

Mother's dark eyes shone warmly as she looked from one boy to the other. "They're growing so fast," she said. "If they feel crowded now, it will be worse later on. Unless we do something about it. I may as well be sensible, and I hope that will stop the argument."

"It should." Father looked very pleased. Joel didn't know whether to feel glad or sorry. He only knew that a change was coming.

"Alex," said Father to the tall boy, "how would you like a room to yourself?"

Alex's face lit up. His blue eyes glistened, though they didn't seem to see anyone. They were full of his own thoughts. "I'd like it," he said slowly. "Thanks, Ma. Thanks, Dad."

Phil was upset. He bit his lip, as if to control himself. Joel had the feeling that Phil might even cry. Soon he straightened up and said quickly, even angrily, to Alex: "But if you go into a room by yourself—in that little *tiny* room—it will spoil everything we were going to do! You can't set up your experiments in a dinky place like that. And if you come up to the big room to do anything, we'll be crowded again—just the way we are now. So what's the use? Besides, why should Ma give up what *she* wants to do?"

"But I want you boys to be comfortable," Mother said. "We have a house now; and if it's my home, it's your home too."

Alex looked undecided. Phil went close to him and talked softly so that Joel couldn't hear what they were saying. Only Phil's last sentence reached him, hotly pleading: "Don't leave me to bunk with that messy kid!"

Joel caught his breath, he was so hurt. He looked around at Mother and Father, hoping they would speak up for him. But they, too, were whispering with the older boys.

Before he had time to say anything, however, Joel saw the group break up. Mother leaned back in her rocker. Alex and Phil stood hand in hand. Father called to Joel: "Well, young fellow, your brothers want to stay in the big room. That means you can have the little room next to ours all to yourself. How's that?"

Joel's mouth dropped open in surprise. "Fine!" he said, very happily, when he was able to speak.

Father slapped him on the back, Mother hugged him, and the other boys laughed at his pleased expression.

To have a room of his own was a step up, Joel

felt. It made him, somehow, seem more important. He would be free, there, to do as he pleased and nobody could get in his way.

It was a little like being promoted. Or was it . . . rather like being left back? He still remembered the hurt to his pride when Phil had called him "that messy kid."

He didn't like being called that, even if it had won him the new room. That his own brothers should think that way of him troubled him all through school the next day. It rubbed in the sad fact that they didn't want a "kid" with them. How long would it be before they thought of him as a grown boy like themselves?

That evening Joel knocked on the door of the living room, where Father was working alone. "Can I ask you something, Pop?"

Father was planning a lesson for next day, but he looked up, fountain pen in hand, as Joel's head came around the door. "If it can't wait until later, you may," he said.

"No. I don't want anyone to hear me."

"Come on in, then." Father put down his pen and, taking up his pipe, relighted and puffed on it. "What's bothering you, son?"

"Isn't there something I can do to grow up faster?" Father took the pipe from his mouth. "Not like eating cereal," Joel added hastily, "or drinking milk, or going to bed on time."

Father thought awhile. "Yes," he said, "there is." Joel listened eagerly. "By the time people grow up," said Father, "they have learned that they have to finish a thing, once they begin it."

"Even if they're tired of it?" Joel puckered his lips as if he were taking medicine.

Father nodded.

"Even if they want to do something else *much* more?" Joel pleaded.

"Yes," Father said. "That's a part of growing up. If you realize it now, that will put you ahead. Unfinished work doesn't count."

"O.K. Thanks, Pop." Slowly Joel withdrew and slid the door closed behind him.

Now he had something to go by. This was Monday night—too late to do anything except think. But Tuesday, after school, Joel went upstairs to the big room—he hadn't moved out of it yet—and completed the derrick he had started to build two weeks ago with Phil's erector set. He tested it by hoisting, first, a package of chewing gum on the crane, then a load of marbles knotted in his handkerchief. It was working well. He had built it properly. Now he took it apart and put it away in the box, together with the pile of spare pieces that had littered the floor below one of the windows all that time.

Wednesday he took his modeling set off the window sill and went to work on the lump of plasticine

that had a pony's head and arching neck and prancing forelegs sticking out on one side. From the
shapeless part of the lump he made the pony's
body and gave it prancing hind legs and a flowing
tail.

"That will look nice in your room," Mother said.

On Thursday, Joel carefully pasted up the cardboard circus scene, with its clowns, its wild-animal
cages and its performers all in place. This, too,
would be an ornament to his new room.

On Friday he opened his paint box, cleaned
away the dried paint from the palette and tubes
and washed the brushes. Then he finished coloring
the blue jays on their flowering spray, and not until

that old page was completed did he turn over a new leaf in his painting book. Next he tinted the robin perched on a garden fence. These two pictures could decorate one of his walls.

On Saturday, feeling more grown-up already, he moved down to his own room. There wasn't much furniture in it besides his cot, but he didn't mind that. The old desk that had been bought for Alex

when he first went to school, and the bookcases that had held *Mother Goose* and fairy-tale books, were getting a new coat of brown enamel. Father let Joel help paint them.

The room had only one window, but that was

very sunny. Mother had hung up curtains of green-and-white check, and she had covered two cushions with the same material for the small wooden armchair.

The room looked cheerful. "Try to keep it neat," said Mother.

Joel liked having a place of his own. No one could shout at him: "Watch out for those slides!" or "Don't lose my place in that book!" At the same time, he wasn't alone here. His parents were next door, while just across the hall were Grandpa's room and the room shared by Sally and Aunt Millie.

But Joel *did* feel lonely. He was shut off from his brothers—and by their own wish.

Soon he heard some news that made him feel even lonelier. Aunt Millie was leaving them. She was going to be married. There wasn't a chance that he might have been told this by mistake, for Aunt Millie and Mr. Epstein gave him the news themselves.

"Joel, you're the first one to know," Aunt Millie told him.

"Yes," said Joel; then, because he supposed he ought to say it, he said: "Thanks."

Mr. Epstein asked pleasantly: "Can you use an extra uncle?"

Joel found his tongue. "I've got other uncles," he said, almost in a whisper, "but I've only got one Aunt Millie."

"I agree with you," the gentleman said. "She is quite special. I don't know anybody else like her."

Silence fell. "But I'm not taking her away, not really," Mr. Epstein went on. "We'll be living just a few blocks away, in the apartment house down the road, and you must come to see us whenever you want to."

That sounded a little better. She would be within reach, at least. Joel looked up at him. "Yes, Mr.—"

"Uncle Dave," Aunt Millie put in coaxingly, and gave Joel a sweet smile.

"Uncle Dave," Joel said, to please her.

"And I'm not leaving before we finish *Tom Sawyer*," she said. "Maybe we'll even get started on *The Prince and the Pauper*."

But that only reminded Joel how much he would miss the pleasant times when he sat close to Aunt Millie, following the printed words and getting to know them as she read.

"Maybe she'll read to both of us," Mr. Epstein suggested. "How will that be?"

Joel nodded. He knew it wouldn't be the same; but, feeling that he ought to be fair, he said: "I can't blame you for wanting her. I want her myself."

They both laughed at that. Uncle Dave took him gently by both shoulders. Aunt Millie leaned down and kissed him.

When they were all three seated on the couch,

Aunt Millie said: "Joel, I was keeping one thing for a surprise, but I think I'll tell you now. For my wedding you're going to have a new suit." In answer to his look of gladness that had a question in it, too, she added: "You can pick it out yourself. Grandpa Mendoza will take you to buy it."

"How about pockets?" Joel asked.

"You can have as many as you want—if they make that many."

Joel turned to Uncle Dave. "How many pockets have *you* got?"

Uncle Dave passed his hands over his gray tweed suit, showing the pockets. "Three in the jacket. Two more in the lining. Four in the pants."

"I want nine pockets," said Joel.

CHAPTER SEVEN

THE NEW GAME

Joel's new suit didn't have nine pockets, but it had seven—which was two more than he had ever had before. It was a gray tweed. Grandpa Mendoza let him pick it himself.

The salesman had said: "Isn't that a little old-looking? Wouldn't the young man like something more cheerful? We're selling a lot of cadet blue." He showed a suit with anchors embroidered on the pocket flaps.

Joel said firmly: "No, thank you. I like this." Grandpa merely smiled and nodded.

After paying for the gray suit, Grandpa took Joel to have some ice cream. Then they went to see *The Wizard of Oz*. They enjoyed the afternoon very much.

Joel wore his new suit for the first time on the Shavuoth holiday, which came, this year, early in June. In memory of the first fruits to ripen, which the Hebrew people used to bring as offerings to the

Temple, the synagogue was decorated with flowers and greenery. Joel enjoyed their fresh, sweet scent, and Shavuoth gave him the feeling that summer was almost here.

He knew, too, that this holiday had another meaning. It was the Season of the Giving of Our Law, when his people, newly freed from Egypt, had come to Mount Sinai and received the Ten Commandments and the rest of the Torah, or Law of Moses.

Joel looked at the scroll of the Torah as it lay unrolled on the reading desk before the rabbi, and imagined himself chanting from it on the Sabbath nearest his thirteenth birthday. He made up his mind that, when he should at last reach that wonderful age and become "a son of the commandment," he would try to read his portion of the Torah as beautifully as Alex had done on his *bar mitzvah*. It was a heavenly daydream!

Of course Joel wore his new suit again at Aunt Millie's wedding.

There were many good things to eat, especially the big chunk of wedding cake which Aunt Millie cut for him.

After the fuss and excitement of the wedding, the house seemed very quiet. Breakfast and supper were less cheerful meals without Aunt Millie. Sally helped Mother with the dishes now, but the promotion didn't please her. Joel offered to help Sally by washing glasses, in addition to his old job of drying and polishing the silver.

Unhappily a soapy glass slipped from his hand while he was rinsing it, and broke against the edge of the sink.

"Sally, you wash them yourself," said Mother. "You want to grow up and wear lipstick. You might as well learn to be handy in the kitchen. That's part of growing up too."

"He broke it," grumbled Sally. "You don't blame him!"

"Because he's trying," said Mother. "I'll say that for him, Joel always tries."

Joel put away the knives and forks and spoons in their tray and went upstairs to Grandpa's room. Thinking how he missed Aunt Millie, he realized that Grandpa, too, must be lonely.

The old man was sitting quite still. His newspaper lay on his knees, but he wasn't reading it. At the sound of footsteps he smiled suddenly, as if waking from a daydream, and pulled Grandma's rocker nearer for his visitor.

Joel settled in it comfortably. "Grandpa, when we went to Grandpa Jacobs' house Passover week, they asked me to read the Four Questions in Hebrew, and they were very pleased. Grandpa Jacobs said I had a Spanish accent. What did he mean?"

"Jews who came from Spain or Portugal" said

Grandpa, putting his newspaper aside, "have a different way of pronouncing Hebrew from the Russian and German Jews."

"Which way is right?" Joel asked.

The old man laughed a little. "We think we're right. They think they're right. No one can prove it. But in Israel, today, they speak Hebrew with the Sephardic, or Spanish, accent."

"We come from the Spanish Jews?"

"Yes. The Mendozas were *hidalgos*—that is, noblemen—back in Spain, about four hundred and fifty years ago, and very wealthy. We were friends of the King's adviser, Don Abarbanel." Grandpa looked up at a framed picture on the wall nearby. It was yellow with age, but it showed very clearly the head and shoulders of a bright-eyed gentleman with a flowing beard and a skullcap on his head.

"Is that Don Abarbanel?"

Grandpa nodded. "Don is a Spanish title. At that time it was like 'lord' or 'sir.' Our ancestor, Leon Mendoza, had this engraving made from a portrait of Don Isaac Abarbanel. He was a great man—a great man . . ." Grandpa paused, lost in thought.

"Is there a story about him?"

"A very interesting story."

"Tell me." Joel tucked his feet under him and, leaning his elbow on the arm of the chair, rested his cheek on his hand.

"You've heard of King Ferdinand and Queen Isabella of Spain?" Grandpa began.

"She's the one who pawned her jewels so Columbus could discover America?"

"It wasn't quite like that," Grandpa smiled, "but you have the right queen.

"In her day—while she and Ferdinand ruled—there lived this learned Spanish Jew, Don Isaac Abarbanel, who wrote books about the Bible. He was also very wise in world affairs. He knew several languages, and was such a charming, pleasant person that he became a favorite at the Spanish court. The King and Queen asked his help in managing the treasury of their country, and were very pleased with the way he did it. They took his advice in everything—except one thing.

"In that one thing they were planning to follow the wish of the priest Torquemada. He told them that the Spanish people couldn't be proper Christians unless all the Jews were driven out of Spain.

"Now Queen Isabella was very religious. She thought her priest knew, better than she, what was right for a Christian queen to do. So she hardened her heart against the Jews, who had lived in Spain hundreds of years and had always been loyal subjects. She persuaded her husband, King Ferdinand, to have them expelled.

"Then they told Don Abarbanel about it. The Queen said graciously: 'But we don't mean this for *you,* Don Abarbanel! You are our friend. You shall stay.'

"And King Ferdinand added: 'What should I do without Don Judah, my skillful physician? I couldn't live without *him!*' Don Abarbanel's eldest son, Judah, was a famous doctor and took care of the King's health.

"What do you think Don Abarbanel said? He was pale as death. He replied: 'I thank your Majesties for your kindness to me. But if you drive my people from our beloved Spain—from this dear land, and the homes where we have lived for centuries—do you think that I could remain here and enjoy your favor, as before? No, your Majesties! I go with my people!'

"The King and Queen were amazed. They were full of arguments, trying to persuade Don Isaac to stay. But he only said: 'I beg you to reconsider. Do not sign the decree of expulsion, I pray you!'

"Don Isaac did everything he could to win mercy for his people. But because of Torquemada's power over the Queen, all that Abarbanel could gain for them was a delay of two days from the time decreed for them to go.

"The date of the expulsion was August 2, 1492. Columbus mentions it in his diary. For on August the third, the next day, he started on the voyage during which he discovered America! You know," continued Grandpa, stroking his gray mustache, "another queer thing about this story is that Don Abarbanel had been the first to aid Christopher Columbus with money for the ships and equipment with which he sailed to America. So, without knowing it, he had helped to find a true home for his suffering people!"

Joel drew a deep breath in wonder. "And what about the Queen's jewels?" he asked.

"Oh yes, the jewels!" Grandpa smiled. "Maybe she was ready to pawn them, but she didn't need to. For another distinguished Jew, Luis de Santangel, who had for a long time been telling her how important it was to Spain that Columbus should succeed, lent her three hundred thousand dollars to get him equipment and provisions, and to have the ships made ready.

"And we had a hand in the voyage too. The physician and the surgeon, and three others on board, were Jews. Columbus, who was setting out to find a way of reaching India by sea, wanted an interpreter who could speak to the Indians. Luis de Torres knew Hebrew and Arabic and one or two other Eastern languages. He was taken along as an interpreter.

"So it happened that the first European to set foot in America was the Jew, Luis de Torres, for Columbus sent him ashore to speak with the natives and tell them their ships were friendly and had come to trade.

"Of course he didn't know their language, or where he really was. But he gave them presents and made friends with them, and brought back gifts from their chief—birds, and beadwork, and fruit that the seamen had never tasted before. And it is told of Luis de Torres that he saw a big bird with a spread tail. He thought it was a peacock. So he called it by the Hebrew word for peacock, which is *tukki*.

"And that's how the turkey got its name!"

Joel laughed and stretched his legs. He had been sitting so still with his feet tucked under him that they had "gone to sleep." While Grandpa rubbed the "pins and needles" out of them, Mother called upstairs: "Joel, it's bedtime!"

"Thanks, Grandpa; that's a wonderful story." Joel sighed with pleasure. "How did our family come to America?" he asked as he stood up.

"The Mendozas? They first went to South America, to the Dutch colony in Brazil. But the Spaniards defeated the Dutch and captured their colony. So the Jews, who had fought on the side of their Dutch protectors, fled for their lives to Holland. Later, when Jews were allowed to settle again in England, the Mendozas went to England.

"Then, in the reign of George II, a law was passed that allowed Quakers, other Protestants and also Jews to become citizens after living in the American colonies for seven years. That was what we wanted! To belong somewhere! So the Mendozas came back to the New World.

"We made our home in New York, and here we've lived ever since. In 1776 we went to Philadelphia with Dr. Seixas, our cantor, and most of the congregation. There we were able to help the Revolution, and we didn't come back until the British were defeated."

"Fine!" cried Joel.

"Get ready for your shower, Joel," Mother called again.

"Just a minute, Ma!" Joel pleaded. "I want to ask Grandpa one more question."

"Oh, you're with Grandpa," said Mother. "That's different."

"Just the same, you have to get up early for school," Grandpa said, putting his arm around Joel's shoulder. "So make it quick."

Glad to delay his bedtime, Joel said slowly and thoughtfully: "But Grandma Mendoza wasn't Spanish, was she? Where did she come from?"

"Peace be upon her! Her family came from Germany about 1830. That's when the German Jews began to arrive. They came because they had heard that, in America, Jews and Christians were treated alike and had an equal chance."

Grandpa was gently leading Joel toward the door. Joel turned and, examining the buttons on Grandpa's waistcoat, asked another question:

"Grandpa Jacobs came from Russia. When did *his* folks get here?"

"Near the end of last century. In Russia, under the Tsars, the Jews were treated very cruelly. At the same time they weren't allowed to leave the country. So they had to escape across the border, bribing officers to let them get away. Many of them had no money left by the time they got here."

Joel nodded. "Thanks," he said.

"Good night!" Grandpa reminded him.

Joel hugged Grandpa, and then slowly, slowly went downstairs to tell Mother he was going up to take his shower and go to bed.

All night Joel dreamed that he was on the ship with Columbus. When he stepped ashore, Alex and Phil were Indians and called him "Turkey."

Alex was very happy these days. He was graduating at the head of his class. And because he had earned the best marks, he was given the highest honor a graduate can have. He was to speak the final speech at graduation, saying good-by to the school for his whole class. He was to be valedictorian.

Alex wrote and rewrote his speech. He read it aloud and practiced speaking it at home until everyone thought it perfect. Joel was never tired of listening to it. He knew it by heart, himself, except that he stumbled over some of the long words. Alex called him, in fun, "My Public."

Joel was so proud of Alex that it hurt him deeply when his big brother did the kind of thing he, Joel, hated most. This is how it happened.

Always good at English, Alex brought home a composition his teacher had praised very much and had kept for several months. It had been read to the class and they all enjoyed it. So he read it aloud to the family one evening when supper was over. The subject was "A Person I Have Known." Alex had chosen to write about "My Little Brother."

Joel sat up, full of interest. He felt flattered that Alex should write about him. As he listened to the composition, however, he began to feel hot and uncomfortable. He was so embarrassed he didn't know which way to look. For all the silly stories he had hoped were forgotten, forever, had been put on paper and read to the older boys and girls in Alex's class and to the teacher, so they could laugh at him.

Nobody else seemed to mind. Father and Grandpa were smiling. Mother and Sally laughed and applauded. Phil was fairly rolling on the floor with glee.

Joel slipped out by the back way. He stumbled down the porch stairs and threw himself on the grass.

Everything was in that composition. How, when

he was five years old, he had come to his big brother and said solemnly: "Alex, yesterday has went." The even sillier one about when he had just learned to walk, and would lie down on the floor in front of a grown-up person and say: "Pick it up me!" Worst of all, how he'd been sitting in his high chair, before he could talk, and had suddenly spoken his first word, which was "Fishy-cooky." His sister and brothers had been so delighted that this had been Joel's nickname for one or two years. Then, luckily, the joke wore out and was forgotten. Now the whole mess had been remembered, all over again!

Joel hid his face in the grass and felt as if he never wanted to get up. But presently he wasn't thinking about the baby stories any more. He was remembering the story Grandpa had told him a few days ago, the story of Don Abarbanel. Those had been real troubles that Don Abarbanel had!

Joel stood up and walked about the lawn. He saw it all happening. Don Abarbanel, hearing the awful news, was standing shocked and silent before the King and Queen.

"We don't mean it for *you*, Don Isaac," Joel repeated in a sweet, queenly voice. "You must stay and be our friend as always."

Don Abarbanel answered. Joel's hand was on his breaking heart; then he stretched out both arms, pleading to the King and Queen: "Oh, have mercy on my people! Where shall we go, if you drive us out?"

"But *you* needn't go," said the Queen's voice again, when Joel, looking down as if from the steps of a throne, turned to face Abarbanel. . . .

Joel was suddenly quiet and still as a statue. Someone had come into the garden.

It was only Sylvia. "Hello," he said.

Sylvia asked respectfully: "Who were you talking to, Joel?"

"Why? Did you hear me?"

"Oh yes," she said. "I've been listening to you. It's thrilling."

"It really happened," said Joel briskly. "Sit down and I'll tell you about it."

Her eyes were very big as she listened, and they never left Joel's face for an instant.

When the story ended, she jumped up. "Let *me* say what the Queen says," she demanded. "You can't be everyone."

That seemed reasonable. Sylvia was the Queen. Having the two of them made it so much more interesting and alive that they went on to the Columbus story. But, with that, they didn't do so well. More players were needed.

"It's too late now," said Joel regretfully. "Otherwise I'd get Leo and Jerry."

"Let's try again tomorrow," Sylvia said eagerly. "Tomorrow, right after school."

But the next day Joel got interested in racing Leo and Jerry. Then they played marbles until Jerry had won everything. In his garden they played at circus. Joel stood on his head—against

the house wall. Jerry turned somersaults. Leo was a clown. Gracie put on the costume she wore in ballet class and danced on a soapbox, which was supposed to be the back of a galloping horse. They finished with roller-skating.

On the day after, however, Joel brought the boys to his house. They acted the Columbus story, beginning with a speech from Joel as the Admiral trying to get men to sail with him over the unknown sea.

They enjoyed it very much.

Sunday morning, when Joel came down to breakfast, Phil and Alex were already stealing out of the house. This was the first Sunday of the summer vacation, when they had no Hebrew School. They were going to Prospect Park with their new "gang" and, clearly, they didn't want Joel along.

Joel's heart thumped heavily. He felt as if he had tasted something bitter. But he was too old, now, to run after them, crying; and too proud to try and "tag along."

He'd show them he didn't care!

CHAPTER EIGHT

THE FRIEND OF THE
INDIANS

Just the same, Joel didn't know what to do with himself. It was too early to call for Leo or Jerry. Mother had warned him that Sunday morning is a quiet time. One shouldn't disturb the neighbors.

"Why don't you do some weeding?" Mother suggested.

Joel weeded the flower bed. He showed his little pile of weeds to Mother, who thanked him and told him to drop them in the waste can.

Then he went upstairs, hanging onto the banister, placing his feet on the steps ahead of him and pulling his body up by grasping at the rails. He was wondering, would it be too early to knock on Grandpa's door?

By the time he reached the landing, the question was answered. Grandpa's door was open and he was getting ready to hang something on the wall of his room.

"Hello, Grandpa!" Joel said gladly. "Can you —" He was going to add "tell me a story?" But he said instead: "Have you had breakfast yet?"

"Hello, Joel." Smiling, Grandpa put down what he was holding to pinch Joel's cheeks. "I had my breakfast before any of you, and I'll tell you a story if you like. I was just remembering one—about these things."

He took up a small Indian rug, and a peculiar long black pipe. The rug was black and white, with here and there a line of bright blue. A zigzag of scarlet and black darted across it from corner to corner. The pipe was of black wood, beautifully made. On its thick, squarish stem a bird with powerful outspread wings was carved. The wings were inlaid with bits of greenish-blue shell, glossy as mother-of-pearl.

"Where did you get these, Grandpa?"

"Oh, I've had them a long time; but, you know, in an apartment there isn't room for everything, so you haven't seen them till now. My grandfather left them to me. He inherited them from his friend John Levy. And how Levy got them—well, that's the story. My grandfather told it to me when I was just about your age.

"In the old days there were big, beautiful stretches of land that white men had never seen. My grandfather Ephraim Mendoza, like other young men of the time, dreamed about going West someday to seek his fortune. He and his best friend, John Meyer Levy, were planning to set out as soon as they were eighteen. But John had a chance to go earlier. Ephraim, who was the eldest son of a big family, had to stay behind and help his parents. However, they kept up their friendship by writing to each other; and Ephraim got a share of John's adventures that way.

"He read how John arrived at St. Louis—a fine city even then, and growing fast—and how he met a German girl named Augusta, whom he married a year later. They moved on to Prairie du Chien in Wisconsin Territory, and then to La Crosse. By this time they had a three-year-old son, Willie. There were only four other white families living at La Crosse when the Levys came there. It was mostly an Indian settlement.

"John began trading with the Indians. He was very successful. The Indians, who were Winnebagoes, liked him. He became a regular Indian agent, giving all his time to their affairs.

"The Winnebagoes had once been an important nation. But nearly half their people had died of smallpox. They believed the disease was brought by the white people. When the Winnebagoes finally settled beside the Mississippi no white people lived there. However, the United States Government wanted to make a state of that part of the country. They promised the Indians land further West, and the Winnebagoes signed a treaty saying they would move on in two years. Now the time had come, and they were heartbroken because they loved their present home.

"Many of the tribesmen urged their chief to ignore the treaty and stay. At a full council around the campfire, they refused to follow him if he and his clan, the Thunderbird, should go.

"But Chief Wakanchara said he had given his word and must keep it. Still he was deeply troubled at the danger to his people. So he sent for John M. Levy and asked his help.

"Meanwhile rumors of the disagreement among

the Indians drifted eastward among the white towns and clearings. The white settlers were afraid. Old stories about Indian raids and massacres were retold, and they filled people's minds with fear.

"On the first of June, Augusta Levy looked out the door and saw about fifty canoes filled with Indian chiefs, dressed in ceremonial robes and paint, with big feather headdresses and tomahawks. She was struck by their beauty, but she forgot about the beauty and was frightened to death at their coming. She and her little son were alone in the house.

" 'They're coming to kill us all!' she cried, and ran about closing shutters and locking doors. Then she grabbed little Willie and they hid in a windowless room.

"It was so still that presently she could hear the sounds of the canoes coming closer and closer. Then the swishing of the paddles stopped. She left her hiding place and went to peep through a loophole in the shutter of a front window.

"The canoes had stopped in front of the house, by the river bank, and the Indians had come ashore. They were marching straight up to her own front door.

"She ran back to the hiding place and covered her ears, to shut out the sound of knocking. They knocked and knocked, but she would not open the door. Then she heard a pounding and, finally, someone kicking at the doors. The noise, she knew, was made not by moccasins but by boots. It almost broke the door down. But still she was too terrified to move.

"The footsteps came around to the kitchen window. A voice called to her: 'Augusta, where are you?'

"It was her husband's voice. Quickly she ran from her corner to let him in. 'Don't you see the Indians around by the front door?' she whispered. 'They're all here, with their tomahawks, to kill us!'

"He seemed not to hear her. 'Open the doors quickly, in heaven's name! What did you lock yourself in for?' he said.

" 'Didn't you see the Indians at the front door, to kill us!' she repeated.

" 'Let me in,' was all he answered. She opened the kitchen door for him. She heard him run through the hall. He opened the front doors.

"Presently he came back. The Indians were filing quietly into the dining room and were seating themselves in ceremonial order on the floor.

" 'I arranged all this,' John explained to his trembling wife. 'This is a council held by the Winnebago chiefs and the heads of the Sioux nation. Wakanchara asked me, as a special favor, to let them hold it in our house. He heard that the white folks have been panicky since the big Camp-fire Council. He hopes it will put an end to the fear, if I give consent to the meeting with the Sioux chiefs under my roof.'

" 'Why didn't you tell me about it?' she demanded. 'Then we wouldn't have been frightened.'

" 'I was so busy with the plans I forgot to tell you,' he admitted, shamefaced. 'I'm sorry!'

" 'Well, you can go wait on them yourself,' she said. 'I'm still shaky.'

"So he took the pail and the pint cup and went down to the river to bring them drinking water. The Levys had no well.

"As he entered with it, Wakanchara asked him to sit with them and hear their new plan. They were willing to give up their present lands to the United States Government, and move immediately. But instead of going far away from the River, to a place they did not know, they would move to the west bank of the Mississippi, to land which they had just purchased from the Sioux nation.

"Wabashaw, head chief of the Sioux, nodded gravely in agreement with everything that Wakanchara said. They begged him to write a letter to Washington asking the Government to take back the treaty.

"Levy promised to do all he could. He smoked the peace pipe with them as it went around the circle, and thought about what he must write. Then the chiefs shook hands with him and took their leave. Augusta appeared in the front hall and wished them a pleasant journey.

"Levy wrote the letter that very night, addressing it 'to the President of the United States, or to the Secretary for Indian Affairs.'

"He wrote that the Winnebagoes had sworn brotherhood with the Sioux nation, and begged to be allowed to take possession of the land they had just purchased from the Sioux. They faithfully promised they would remain away from the east bank, and never harm any of the white citizens. More than that, they would defend the property and lives of the whites against any interference from other Indians. In everything they would be 'forever governed by the President's wise consideration' and 'be ever ready to obey the command of the Government of the United States.'

"Levy himself rode to Madison, in order to send the letter safely on its way.

"Then there were days of anxious waiting. It was very quiet at La Crosse. Most of the traders had already left for the new Northwest country that was later to become Minnesota. But Wakanchara and his people still remained. After sunset John and Augusta and their white neighbors heard the Indian women singing—lullabies, love songs, songs that went with playing games. Sometimes a beautiful, clear voice sounded above all the others. It was the voice of Summer Sky, Wakanchara's wife.

"As time passed and there was still no word from Washington, there came a change in the singing.

Only one person sang, Summer Sky, and she was singing a new song. It was a lovely, sweet song, but so sad it was more like a wail. It made Augusta, mending by lamplight in her homey kitchen, shudder and wipe tears from her eyes. John, reading his two-week-old newspaper, had to stop and clean his glasses.

"They said the song haunted them ever after. On a quiet night, or when alone or sad, they would hear again, in memory, that lovely voice singing what seemed like a farewell.

"At last, when nearly a month had passed, the letter came. Levy tore it open.

"It was a stern note from the Secretary for Indian Affairs, warning Levy that 'no such schemes can be countenanced for a moment'; and that he must not interfere in any way with the removal of the Indians as planned, or he would be subject to punishment under the law.

"Downhearted, he set out for the Indian village. Augusta tried to cheer him, saying: 'Summer Sky knew that it would end this way. You could hear it in her singing. It won't shock them too much.'

"When he arrived, Wakanchara knew the answer before Levy could speak. He called his chieftains and ordered a feast and games.

"When Levy rose to go, they gave him parting gifts. Wakanchara presented him with this pipe on which was carved the Thunderbird, his emblem.

Summer Sky had woven this rug with her own hands; and had also made a pair of deerskin moccasins embroidered with porcupine quills, for little Willie.

"Levy was touched. 'But I brought you bad news!' he said. 'I wasn't able to help you.'

" 'You are our friend,' said Wakanchara peacefully. 'May the Sun, the Moon, and the Morning Star shield you forever.'

"That year, 1848, Wisconsin became a state and was admitted to the Union."

Grandpa paused. "That's the way my grandfather told it to me," he said.

"You remember it so well!" Joel exclaimed. "But didn't Great-great-grandfather ever get to see John M. Levy again?"

"Oh yes," said Grandpa. "He went out West to visit him. But that was much later—when Levy was Mayor of La Crosse, the town he built up. The first hotel, the first dock, the first barge for river traffic had been put up by him, and La Crosse was now the county seat. The citizens showed their gratitude by electing him alderman eight times and mayor three times."

Joel helped Grandpa fasten the Indian rug to a panel in the wall, and laid the pipe carefully on the bracket above it.

CHAPTER NINE

THE FRIEND OF THE
SLAVES

That afternoon Joel was in the back garden with Leo, telling him the story of John M. Levy while Sylvia listened from her side of the hedge, when Jerry arrived.

He had been running and, while he opened the gate, he looked behind him as if he were being followed. He threw himself down beside the other two boys in the shade of the oak tree. On his forehead the curly red hair was damp with perspiration. He fanned his face with both hands. "What's doin'?" he asked.

But before Joel or Leo had a chance to answer him, Jerry heard the gate squeak. He turned. "I knew it!" he cried angrily. There was Gracie, leaning on the gate and nibbling at a stalk of grass. He turned back to the boys, complaining loudly: "She's always following me! She's got plenty of girl friends!" Then he turned to Gracie. "Why don't you play with Myrna or Bess?"

"I like your games better," replied Gracie.

"It's all right," Joel assured Jerry. "If we're going to act the story of Columbus, we've got to have a crew." Gracie opened the gate and strolled in. "We need everyone we can get." Joel beckoned to Sylvia.

"When I had the measles," said Joel, "my mother read me a book about Columbus. You know, when they were almost here, some of the crew wanted to turn the ships around and go back home. And the one at the head of the gang said if Columbus wouldn't go back with them they'd throw him overboard to drown. Then they'd go home and say he was dead through an accident. I think that's good to act."

They all jumped up. Joel said, with his hand on Leo's shoulder: "You be the leader of the fellows that want to turn back."

Leo shrugged his hand off. "I don't wanna be a coward!" he exclaimed.

"But it's only pretend," cried Joel.

"Nope. I won't."

"I'll take it," said Gracie.

So they acted out the story. They had such a good time they asked Joel if he knew any others. Joel was so pleased he told them the story of John M. Levy. They acted that, too, and they all agreed

play-acting wasn't silly if it was about real people.

One morning Joel overslept. When he came downstairs the older ones had almost finished breakfast. As he entered the kitchen he could hear them, still seated at the dining-room table, planning the day. All three were going to the Museum of Natural History. It would be Sally's first visit there.

"Wait till you see those monsters!" Alex told her. "Dead for millions of years, yet you can tell how they looked when they were alive."

"They must be awful!" Sally's voice was full of shivers.

"There's one kind with a huge tail, and a little

teeny head on an immense long neck. That's the dinosaur," said Phil.

Joel felt a great longing to see a dinosaur. Quietly he came into the room. "Take me too!" he begged.

His brothers and sister looked at one another, pained. He could see they didn't want to hurt his feelings, but the answer was "No."

"Another time," said Sally soothingly. She went to bring in his orange juice and the cereal which Mother was keeping warm for him.

"You wouldn't be interested in the things we're going specially to look at," Alex remarked.

"It's a great big place," said Philip. "You'd get tired and drag behind us."

"We'd have to watch out for you all the time," Alex continued, "or you'd get lost."

"Just as if I was a baby!" Joel burst out.

But Mother settled the question. "I don't want you to go far from the house today, Joel," she said. "It might rain, and you had a temperature last night."

It did rain in the afternoon. Joel had to stay indoors.

When Grandpa came home about four o'clock, he found Joel waiting for him, sitting on the top step outside his room.

"Ah, I have company!" Grandpa exclaimed. "That's nice! Company." He led the way into his room.

Joel dropped into Grandma's rocker with the

cushioned back. "It's raining, and Mom won't let me go out," he sighed. "Tell me a story."

Grandpa put away his hat and changed his stiff shirt for a soft one and put on an old jacket. "I was thinking," he said as he settled in his own big chair, "about a story my grandmother told me when I was about your age."

"She was my great-great-grandmother?" Joel asked.

"Right," answered Grandpa. "And a pretty young lady she was, in her time." He found an old red velvet-covered photograph album and turned the pages to a dim picture of a smiling girl. "She was Miss Lily Einstein before she married your great-great-grandfather, and while she was growing up she lived in Kansas.

"Kansas, in those days, was the most exciting place in the whole country. And don't forget, Joel, excitement isn't always fun. It can also be a terrible thing.

"As your great-great-grandmother told me, when she and her family first came to Kansas, they never knew what might happen to them. Each night they feared their little house might be burned over their heads before morning. They lived in constant dread that the cows might be stolen and the barn emptied before the next milking time. Added to that was the danger that their father and older brothers might be shot and killed for guarding their possessions.

"Was it Indians?" gasped Joel.

"No, it wasn't Indians," Grandpa replied. "It was the Border Ruffians, as they were called.

"Kansas wasn't a state yet. It wasn't fully settled. The South wanted each new state to join with those where Negroes were held as slaves. The North wanted each new state to be a free state. The Einsteins, and other people who believed that slavery was wrong, came to live in Kansas Territory. They meant to vote "No Slavery" when the new land became a state.

"But right next door to Kansas—the nearest state to the east—was Missouri, a slave state. Across that border came reckless men who thought that, by making life miserable and dangerous for the free-state settlers, they could drive them out of Kansas and force her to become a state that upheld slavery.

"These were the Border Ruffians. They robbed and burned and murdered. Most of the settlers were peaceful people who defended themselves the best way they could. But they weren't doing so well against the Ruffians.

"However, there came to Kansas, all the way from New England, a tall man with six sons. His name was John Brown. He said: 'We will not only fight against the Border Ruffians but will drive *them* out. Kansas shall be free. Our country shall be rid of slavery. It is God's will.'

"Other brave men came to join John Brown,

and soon the Border Ruffians weren't having it all their own way. The youngsters in the Einstein family no longer felt afraid. There was danger; but there was the thrill of fighting back in a good cause, with a chance to win.

"Now in St. Louis, about this time, lived a daring, freedom-loving young man named August Bondi. Before he was fifteen he had fought for the revolution in Austria. When it failed he and his family escaped to the United States. A few months after his arrival in St. Louis he was attending meetings where speakers argued against the spread of slavery.

"Then, one day, he read an appeal in a newspaper, the New York *Daily Tribune,* calling to 'the freedom-loving men of the States to rush to Kansas and save it from the curse of slavery.' August Bondi felt that this was *his* job and his duty.

"Two other men joined him in his new plan. One was Jacob Benjamin, in whose shop he had worked, and the other was big, stout Theodore Weiner. They made their way to Kansas and settled there. They meant to do some farming along with trading and storekeeping. The Einsteins, who were their nearest neighbors—about half a mile away—were glad of their coming.

"They spent the first two or three days after their arrival in unpacking their belongings and arranging the stock in Weiner's store. They were just sitting down to supper in Bondi's cabin, on the third evening, when they heard a tap on the door and then a thump, as if something had fallen against it.

"As Bondi opened it, a skinny young Negro fell across the threshold and lay still. August Bondi felt his own knees weaken and his heart ache. This was his first meeting with a runaway slave.

"Weiner carried the youth to a bunk. Bondi wrung out a bandanna in water and brought it to bathe the boy's face.

"But by that time the boy was sitting up and saying in a sweet, low voice: 'Fer the love o' God, help me!' It was not a boy. It was a girl!

" 'Best thing we can do for you, Miss,' said Benjamin, 'is get some food into you, then take you to the Einsteins. They've got girls in the family. They'll do better at hiding you.'

"She was almost too weak to sit up, and they asked her no questions until the food had strengthened her. She told them her name was Vinnie Grayson.

"Weiner remarked: 'It's hard enough for a boy to head for free soil alone. For a girl, it was much more dangerous!'

" 'But I just couldn't wait,' she said. Her eyes flashed; then tears came into them.

"The men hid her in a potato sack, and brought her on a wheelbarrow to the Einsteins. The eldest daughter, Henrietta, was a grown-up young lady. She promised to take care of Vinnie.

" 'I know what we'll do with her,' she said. 'We'll bring her to the Mannheims. They're going north to Iowa next week, and they'll take Vinnie along.'

"Next morning August Bondi saw Miss Henrietta, with her younger sister, Lily, beside her, driving the horse and buggy along the stony road. The girls were dressed up to go visiting. Henrietta reined in the horses as she saw him.

"Looking down at the woolen rug piled in front of their feet, she said: 'Mr. Bondi, I worked all winter knitting this afghan as a going-away present for the Mannheims. I'm so glad I've finished it in time.'

" 'Congratulations, Miss Einstein!' he smiled. 'I'm sure your cleverness won't be wasted!'

"And so it turned out. Nobody suspected that the two gaily dressed young girls, going on a visit in broad daylight, were hiding in the cramped space under their knitted afghan a girl named Vinnie.

"After that August Bondi and his two partners couldn't wait to get in touch with John Brown. They made their way after nightfall to his house and asked to join his band.

"The tall old man looked them over with his sharp, understanding eyes. 'This may cost you your lives,' he said.

" 'We know,' said Weiner.

" 'And you're offering your lives?' Old Brown smiled faintly. 'Why?'

" 'We're Jews,' said August Bondi, and he quoted from the Passover Haggadah: 'Slaves were we unto Pharaoh in Egypt.'

" 'Good!' cried John Brown, and he shook hands with each of them.

"They went with Brown to a hiding place chosen for his headquarters. Here free-state settlers came to join them or to bring reports.

"Bondi and his friends got to know John Brown and to love him. He was like a father to his volunteers, interested in every one of them and kind in little ways. He cooked meals for them out of any food that the Free Staters sent. He noticed that Bondi's shoes were soon worn through and his bare toes were bleeding from the stones and thorns. Brown gave him the next pair of boots that turned up.

"About ten days after their coming to Brown's camp, a neighbor brought news for Bondi and his friends. The Ruffians had burned down August's cabin, stolen his cattle, and robbed Weiner's store. 'Now they'll learn to respect other people's property!' their leader had shouted, shaking his clenched fist. 'That'll teach them not to hide runaways!'

" 'It didn't take them long to find out!' Bondi

sighed. But he was very glad the Einsteins had not been suspected for their part in Vinnie's escape.

"Those were wild months. Captain Brown's forces were never very long in any one place. When not fighting, they were hiding. They moved by night.

"August Bondi never forgot the Battle of Black Jack. A band of the Border Ruffians was encamped in a grove of oak trees on a hill. At the foot of the hill was the old wagon trail of the Santa Fe road. It had been washed out by rains, so it was two feet deep.

"Captain Brown used this as a rifle pit. He ordered his men to lie down in it, and fire whenever they could hit the enemy. But, watching through a spyglass, he noted that one by one the Missourians were slipping away.

"'We mustn't let them escape,' he said. With Bondi, Weiner and two other men, Brown went up the hillside at the back of the Missourian camp. 'If we're bold enough,' he said to his company, 'they'll think we have many more coming behind us!'

"He charged down the hill, straight toward Captain Pate, the leader, with Bondi and the three others dashing after him. Aiming at Pate's heart with his revolver, Brown cried: 'Unconditional surrender!'

"His bold plan succeeded. The Ruffians dropped their rifles. Pate gave up his sword.

"Another time they were raiding the proslavery settlement at Sugar Creek, and the greatest thrill of that raid was when they found in the bottom of a covered wagon, packed and ready to start south, a beaten-up fugitive.

"They freed him from the bruising ropes, wrapped him in a blanket and got him ready to leave with them.

"When the fighting in Kansas ended, Bondi married Miss Henrietta; and by the time their first child was born, the Civil War had broken out.

"Bondi's mother said to him: 'I'll take care of your wife and child, my son. You do as you have always done—defend those institutions that give equal rights to all beliefs.'

"He enlisted in the Union army and became First Sergeant of Company K of the Fifth Kansas Volunteer Cavalry. He served for three years, until he was dangerously wounded and discharged from the army."

"Did he die?" demanded Joel.

"Bless you, no. He lived to be seventy as a Kansas farmer. He and Henrietta had ten children, and he was several times honored by election to public office in his district.

"Lily became a nurse during the Civil War, and that's how she met your great-great-grandfather. They married and he brought her back home with him to New York."

Next morning the weather was fine. Joel and his

friends tried out the August Bondi story. It was harder than the others because you needed more characters. But they liked it because each boy in turn was allowed to act John Brown or August Bondi, and Gracie was either Miss Henrietta or Vinnie. Sylvia gladly took whichever part they left for her.

There were hot days when Joel went to the beach with his family, or on picnics or boat rides. Other times, if he wanted to play regular games, he went to call for Jerry and Leo. But when they came to Joel's house, it meant they were in the mood for acting. It was a lively summer, full of fun and friendship.

Presently Joel found that when Philip and Alex ran off to the park, or the swimming pool, or the library, without him, it didn't matter so much.

He was too busy to care.

CHAPTER TEN

JOEL TO THE RESCUE

One afternoon Leo was going on an errand for his mother. He asked Joel along for company.

"Let's play 'Skin the Cat' on the way," Joel suggested. He took a stick about two feet long, and a chip of wood sharpened evenly at both ends, which was the 'cat.' It made the distance seem much shorter, to play a game as they went along.

On the way back, when they were a few blocks from home, they ran into an adventure.

Sally was leaning against a store window and crying. The store window was very dusty, and for Sally not to notice that meant she must really be in trouble. "What's the matter, Sis?" Joel asked.

She turned her flushed, streaky face halfway toward him. "I'm such a dope!" she cried. Joel realized that Sally must be very miserable to say such a thing in front of anyone younger than herself.

He frowned in sympathy. "What did you do? Maybe we can help you?"

"No. You're too little," she said hopelessly.

Joel was hurt, but still he felt sorry for her. "How do you know we can't?" he insisted.

"Remember 'The Lion and the Mouse'?" put in Leo, twisting his cowlick.

"That was only a story!" Sally moaned. But she did tell them that Mrs. Simmons, who had been visiting at their house the day before, had dropped the key to her mailbox. "We found it under the fringe of the carpet, after she went home. Mother gave it to me to bring to Mrs. Simmons. And I had it in my pocket, here." Her hand tugged at the patch pocket, shaped like a red apple, on her gingham dress ."And I was going along like this—" She illustrated with a hop and a skip. "And it fell right out of my pocket and down the grating! There it is!"

Between the bars of the iron grating under their feet, Joel could see a tiny flat key of metal. He glanced quickly at the shop. It was a plumbing-supply store, one of those that seem never to be open. You couldn't get down to the cellar by the basement stairs.

"Isn't it just maddening!" Sally cried, closing her hands into fists.

"Well, it's not your fault," said Joel. "You didn't mean it."

"But Mother trusted me," Sally sobbed. "And she phoned Mrs. Simmons that I was bringing it.

And now I'll look like a fool in front of Mrs. Simmons and—and—Jack Simmons."

A quick pain went through Joel's chest. He knew that fear quite well—the fear of looking foolish. "We'll get it for you. Don't worry," he said briskly.

Dropping to the sidewalk away from the grating, Joel emptied his pockets. His pack of baseball players, held by a rubber band, came out first. Then a net-bag of marbles, a handkerchief, a caster from an old chair leg, a puzzle in which the teeth of a lion had to be rolled into place, some sticks of chewing gum, two or three sourballs working out of their cellophane twists, a watch spring and two watch wheels, a brass button, a shirt button, four or five rubber bands of different sizes, several paper clips, a large safety pin, three coils of string, a burned-out fuse, a pocket flashlight, two stubs of pencil, an ink eraser, a grimy little pad with a scrap of carbon paper, and a tiny china dog.

Of course the horseshoe magnet he had been looking for was the last thing to be found! Joel tied the little horseshoe to the end of a string and let it down between the bars of the grating.

Leo got down on his hands and knees to watch. Sally leaned over anxiously. She gasped when the magnet stuck to the key. But it didn't quite lift it from the ground. As soon as Joel drew on the string, the key dropped off.

After several tries he coiled up the cord and said, shaking his head: "This calls for . . ." He held out his left hand to Leo, for the proper word.

"In-gen-u-i-ty," Leo supplied. He loved long

words and spoke them as if every syllable tasted good.

"Thanks, pal!" said Joel. He took the stick with which they'd been playing "Cat," fastened his strongest cord to one end and stuck his chewing gum on the other.

Carefully he passed the stick between two bars

and let down the cord, little by little, until it reached the ground. Then, kneeling on the grating, he tried to bring the stick exactly above the key. But the stick flipped aside, or swung away, just when he had it in place.

Still he kept on trying. He tried a different sort of movement. He dipped the stick up and down on the ground, as near the key as possible, feeling for it. Presently he felt a tiny jerk on the cord in his hand and, when the stick came up and away, the key wasn't there on the cellar paving any more!

"I've got it," Joel breathed. The bars were cutting into his knees by now, but he didn't dare change his position. Slowly, slowly, he rolled the cord around his fingers. . . .

"Can you get it through the grating?" Sally said tensely.

Joel drew in the string even more carefully. The top of the stick was only a foot from the grating. They could see the handle of the key sticking out past the gum. The stick might swing, passing through the bars and jerk off the gum with its burden. The slightest movement, now, might loosen the key so it would fall again. . . .

Nobody breathed.

At last Joel's left hand could reach the top of the stick. With patient care he raised it until it was above the bars. Sally's hand was already below the little key. She seized it with a shout of joy. Then both her arms went around Joel, and she hugged him as he struggled to his feet.

"Thanks a million, Joel!" said Sally. "You're so smart!" While he rubbed his dented knees, she pushed the hair back from her face. "I bet I look awful," she said happily, and ran homeward to tidy up before starting out once more for the Simmons house.

There was a window on the stairway in the hall from which you could see the garden and everything that happened in it. Twice in the week that followed, Joel noticed that Sally was watching him and his friends from behind the curtain. He didn't know whether to feel pleased or worried. Of course it was flattering to have his big sister show such interest in what he and his gang were doing. But perhaps she was laughing at him? And she might tell Phil and Alex, and they would laugh too.

Joel wasn't kept long in doubt. Sally soon appeared in the back garden, openly watching them. They were acting the Columbus story and Sylvia, as Queen Isabella, was sending the Admiral of the Ocean on his way.

"Wait a minute," Sally called to Sylvia, walking to the middle of the lawn. "You'd look more like a queen if you wore a crown and a robe—some sort of costume, anyway."

Silence fell. Sally's voice was quite serious. While

Joel wondered what she meant by interfering, Sylvia answered for all of them. "We do what *Joel* says. Joel began it." The little girl's eyes, full of admiration, were turned on Joel.

Sally, too, looked at Joel as though she were seeing him for the first time. "It would be nice," she said, "with costumes. I could fix you some." Sally's eyes had their excited look—like blue fire. Her voice was serious.

"But you won't—" he began doubtfully.

"Tell the others? Not if you don't want me to," she promised firmly. "And I'd—I'd sure like to act."

"We need more characters," said Joel, delighted. "You could be—"

"I could be Vinnie Grayson, that escaped slave," she put in quickly.

"But you're so blond!"

"What does that matter, if we're going to dress up for the parts?"

Sally brought new surprises into their already fascinating play. She made little Sylvia a lovely train of wine-red brocade. It tied on each shoulder with a gold cord and tassels: Out of cardboard covered with gilt paper, Sally shaped a crown. She edged it with a necklace of pearl beads that Mother didn't wear any more because she had better ones, and at the highest point, center front, she fastened a clip of red garnets. It made a believable crown.

Sally could do this because she was allowed to take any of Mother's finery not now in use. She might also choose whatever she wished out of the old trunk of family treasures. Mother knew that everything would be put back neatly and in the same condition as when it was taken out. For, though she might fold, or drape, or sew on the fine materials she borrowed for her play-acting, Sally never cut or spoiled them in any way.

Nearly every time she had something new for one of the characters to wear. She found buckles for the shoes of King Ferdinand. She made a blue lace hoop skirt for Miss Henrietta, and a striped silk one for Augusta Levy, in the Indian scenes. But her most valuable find was an old fringed tablecloth of crimson damask. It could be draped over both thrones, or it could be Ferdinand's royal robe. It made a tent for Summer Sky and a gorgeous sail for the Admiral's flagship.

Joel couldn't remember having so much fun ever before! And what made it especially wonderful was Sally not acting like a big sister!

One day they were all in the back yard, resting between stories. Out front the older boys were playing ball and Joel had a feeling of warm contentment. There was a sudden shout that startled him, but it was followed by a deep silence. Then he heard Alex say: "I'll get you out, Phil! Take it easy."

Something was the matter. Joel ran to see. Sally and the younger ones came crowding after.

The big boys were grouped around Phil, who was crouching on the ground. He seemed unable to get up. Joel pushed in among them, and from their talk he gathered that Phil had run for the ball which had fallen on a heap of sewer pipes. In hopping over the pile he had fallen and his foot had caught in the opening of the eight-inch pipe.

Alex was grasping Phil under the armpits, trying to jerk him free by main strength. For all the twisting and pulling, the foot was only jammed more firmly. The other boys tried dragging and tugging, but Phil's ankle got redder and more swollen above the sock.

Phil dropped down on the ground. His face was smeary and hot. There was actually a tear streaking out of one eye.

Joel felt terribly sorry for Phil—and for Alex, standing over him, helpless. Stewy, with a mischievous grin, said: "Maybe he'll have to have the foot cut off!"

This was more than Joel could bear. He clenched his fists and shouted: "Would you say that if it was *your* brother?"

"I'll get a hammer and break the pipe!" said Alex desperately. "Joel, you know where the tool kit is—"

Phil gulped. "No, don't do that. It will only get us all in trouble."

"Wait a minute," said Joel. "Which way were you facing, Phil, when your foot got caught?"

"This way." Leaning on Alex, Phil stood up and turned to face the houses.

"Then turn your foot the way it was when it got stuck," said Joel. "I'm sure you can pull it out the same way it got in."

"What's the use?" groaned Phil, sinking down again.

"That's a good notion!" Alex exclaimed. He pulled Phil up, supporting him under the arms. The other boys crowded around to help. They shifted and pushed, a little at a time, with Joel hanging over them, while Phil gritted his teeth and pulled. The foot was released!

A cheerful yell went up.

"Why didn't we think of that ourselves?" said one boy.

"I guess we were too rattled," said Alex. "We lost our heads."

"Gosh! Thanks, fellows!" said Phil, stepping down carefully on the wrenched ankle. He gasped and took his weight off it again. With Alex's arm around him and leaning lightly on Joel's shoulder, Phil hopped into the house.

In the kitchen Mother strapped the foot and ankle with bandages soaked in ice water. "If it isn't

all right tomorrow," she said anxiously, "we'll have the doctor look at it."

All at once Joel felt himself grabbed by the shoulders and pushed forward. "This is the guy you gotta thank!" said Alex warmly.

Phil threw an arm around Joel. Then he shook hands with him, man to man. It made Joel feel at least an inch taller.

CHAPTER ELEVEN

A SHOW FOR GRANDPA

Summer vacation was over. In three more days it would be Succoth, the Feast of Booths. For the first time, the family would be able to build their own *succah,* or little hut, in the back garden. The *succah* was to remind them of the little huts which the Israelites had put up for shelter, while wandering forty years in the wilderness before they could enter the Promised Land.

Phil, the mechanic, the handy man of the family, took charge and did most of the work. Joel stood by, holding hammer and nails, assisting wherever he could. Using the grape arbor in the corner, they had only two walls to put up. The green roof was there already, with enough space between the leaves so that they could see the stars at night.

For the entrance Father helped Phil take a closet door off its hinges and bring it out to the garden, where they fastened it in place.

In three afternoons the *succah* was finished.

Sally took over the decorating. She made paper chains that opened out accordion fashion. Mother brought out fruit. For Succoth, since it was the final harvest festival of the year, is also called the Feast of Ingathering. Sylvia polished the apples and held them up, shiny red, for Sally to fasten to the green roof. With bananas and pears and whatever grape clusters were left, they made the little hut a gay and festive place.

It was jolly, eating their suppers in the *succah*. Sylvia was invited on the first night. She sat next to Joel. Everybody was delighted; and you couldn't say which of them was happiest, Phil, or Joel, or Sally—or perhaps Grandpa and the parents, in their quieter way.

However, in spite of Grandpa's joy at having the *succah,* Joel noticed that at times he seemed very sad. He seemed absent-minded and far away. As soon as supper was over, he excused himself and went upstairs.

Once Joel went up after him. "What's the matter, Grandpa?" he asked.

"Nothing, Sonny," Grandpa patted his shoulder. "A little headache, that's all."

"Are we making too much noise outside?"

"Noise? What noise? I don't even hear you." Grandpa sat down in his chair. "Children have to play." He smiled. "Go and play."

Joel asked Mother about it.

"He's rather lonesome these days," she said. "I guess he misses Grandma. It's getting on toward autumn, and that was the time Grandma died."

"Oh yes!" said Joel, feeling stupid for not having thought of it. Joel told Sally. "I wish," he sighed, "we could think of something to cheer him up."

"Let's both think," said Sally.

It was she who found the way. "We'll put on a show for Grandpa!" she exclaimed. "Let's act everything, right here in the garden. We'll bring out a chair for him to watch."

"Do you think he'd like that?" Joel asked shyly.

"Why wouldn't he?" Sally demanded. "Especially since you got the ideas from the stories he told you. It will please him a lot!" Her blue eyes were alight with eagerness. "Of course we'll have to practice, and get everything ready beforehand, so there will be no stopping in the middle of a scene."

Joel found himself agreeing. It *was* the kind of thing Grandpa Mendoza would like. Joel would enjoy acting the plays for Grandpa. So, too, it turned out, would Sylvia and Gracie.

Jerry was not very pleased with the idea.

"Aw, be a sport!" Leo told him. "It's for Joel's Grandpa."

"O.K.," said Jerry, amiable again. "I don't want to spoil the game."

The next thing Sally told them was less easily settled. She needed some money. The costumes would have to be more complete, now that they were going to act before a grown-up person. There were some things they would have to buy—feathers for the Indian scenes; burlap, to make jerkins for the sailors; sateen and crepe paper and oilcloth for boots.

"Who's got any money?" She glanced doubtfully around the little gathering. Nobody answered. It was only Wednesday; but everybody's allowance was spent, including her own.

"I'll give you my next week's allowance," said Joel, "soon as I get it." He had another thought. "I can ask Mom ahead of time."

"So will I," said Sally. Then she, too, had another thought. "After all"—she turned to the others—"you're doing this to please us. I don't think anyone outside our family should give any money."

"Oh yes, we should," said Gracie proudly.

"No," said Sally, "and that's that!"

Asking for their allowance in advance, Sally and Joel had to take Mother and Father into their confidence. As Sally expected—for she knew her grownups!—they met with good luck. Not only did they get their next week's allowance but they also got a dollar from Father and another one from Mother. They both liked the idea of having a show for Grandpa.

"What are the plays about?" Father asked as he put his wallet away. Mother, too, looked as if she would like to know more about it.

"Look," said Joel, "you come too. Both of you." He glanced at his manager. "It's all right to ask them, isn't it?"

Sally gave her parents an approving nod. "Sure is," she said. "You will sit on each side of Grandpa and keep him company."

Out in the garden again, Joel remarked; "If we have Mom and Dad, I want to invite Aunt Millie too."

"Then you'll have to have Uncle Dave, as well."

"O.K.," said Joel. "They'll sit on one side of Grandpa, and Mom and Dad on the other. Grandpa will like it."

"Let me invite them," suggested Sally.

She did it so well that two more dollars from Uncle Dave were added to the fund. Cleverly, with Mother's help, Sally did her buying. The show was planned for Saturday, two weeks off.

Meanwhile something very interesting happened at a school assembly period. Mr. Adams, the principal, was talking about Brotherhood Week, which comes in February. Then he said: "In our neighborhood we have children from several different national groups, all of which have helped to make our country great. I think it will be a good idea, as we start our school year, if we have our own Brotherhood Week. Perhaps we can make it the last week in October.

"Then we can have an Irish Day, Italian Day, Jewish Day, Negro Day, and Polish and Slavic Day. In its turn each group will remind us, here in assembly, of its contribution to the history of the United States and to our way of life, of which we are so proud."

Joel joined in the loud applause, clapping so hard that his palms were red. Everybody chattered to everybody else until Mr. Adams held up his hand. Then they quieted down again, to hear what more he had to say.

"I've mentioned the names in their alphabetical order," he went on. "So we needn't argue about who's most important or who came first!" There was a burst of laughter, for some of the children had been doing just that. "All of us are important, and we couldn't have done so well with any less. I expect that's what we'll discover, during our Brotherhood Week."

Joel felt this was something exciting to look forward to; and when he and Sally and Philip told their parents about it at suppertime, they, too, felt that the principal's idea was a fine one.

"Talking about ideas," said Alex as he finished his chocolate pudding, "our English teacher's come up with a lulu—"

"And what's *that,* in English?" asked Father, raising one eyebrow.

"A great one. Something new and—live!" Looking around him, Alex joined in the laugh against himself. They were listening attentively, for he was the first to go to high school.

"Well, he's very clever and jolly, this teacher is. All the boys like him. And he says he wants the students to learn to *like* poetry. He wants them to find out for themselves how good it is, to read and know. So he's not giving us a mid-term exam, because he knows the fellows would cram for it and worry about their marks; and that would make poetry a headache. Instead he wants each boy to have a scrapbook and paste in it the twenty-five poems he likes the best. And we'll be marked on the neatness and good taste we show in fixing up our books."

"Excellent," said Father. "I know one student who's going to have fun with it!"

"You bet!" exclaimed Alex, and his face shone with enthusiasm. "I've got all sorts of ideas for my scrapbook. I'm going to have an illustration for each poem. Too bad I can't draw like Sally."

"Thanks, pal." Sally squeezed more lemon juice into her tea.

"But I guess I can find the pictures that fit in. You know, cut them out of magazines and ads."

"Maybe we can help you," suggested Phil.

"That will be fine. I'll pick my poems first, and

read them to you. Then I'll be glad if you find anything for me."

"I'm sure yours will be the best in the whole class!" said Joel.

"I hope it will," said Alex. "I mean to get top marks for it!"

To his delight Joel was the first to discover a good illustration. In a railroad advertisement he found a colored picture of a mountain, with a long waterfall streaming down to a canyon lined with trees and ferns. It would go beautifully with the poem beginning:

> *Up the airy mountain,*
> *Down the rushy glen,*
> *We daren't go a-hunting*
> *For fear of little men.*

He ran to Alex, holding the picture up high.

"Perfect!" said Alex. He measured it carefully against a sheet of paper and marked out the space it would take up. Then he typed the poem in a long, narrow column; and when it was finished, he pasted the picture alongside. It made a very nice page.

After that, Joel always felt he had a share in the scrapbook. Though he had to keep his hands behind him while Alex turned the pages, Joel was very much interested. He watched a green-eyed tiger, with bared teeth and lashing tail, slink through reeds at the head of the poem:

Tiger, tiger, burning bright
In the forests of the night.

Best of all he liked the first page, where a great
ship spread its rose-colored sails before a golden
sunset. This was the illustration for the beautiful, sad poem "O Captain, My Captain!" which
mourns the death of Abraham Lincoln.

Between this and starting geography and learning to multiply at school, and getting ready for
Grandpa's show, the time passed rapidly for Joel.
In a flash, it seemed to him, Saturday afternoon
arrived and it was time for the acting to begin.

More people came than Joel had expected.
Sylvia and Gracie had asked that their parents be
invited. Leo's mother came at the last moment. A
neighbor or two, from further up the street, appeared. Mother and Father were having a few
friends in, later that evening. Somehow the grown-
up audience took up three rows of chairs.

When Joel ran to tap on the living-room door
and call Father, he heard the voice of a lady visitor.
He knew the voice, and yet he couldn't quite re-
call who the speaker was.

"I've been told that you're an expert on Jewish
history and culture," the lady was saying.

"It's very nice that someone thinks so," Father
replied with a chuckle.

"'Scuse me, Pa," Joel called out. "We're ready
to start." Joel ran back to the grape arbor, from

which he and Columbus were to make their entrance.

"You see," she went on, "I hardly know where to begin. So I've come to you for a suggestion."

"You couldn't have come at a better time," said Father. "Here's a suggestion for you!" He led her out to the garden and seated her in the back row of spectators, unseen by the children until the show was over.

It was a great success. The audience clapped, and laughed, and clapped again.

Afterward ice cream was served to the actors, along with big pieces of the layer cake Mother had baked. The older people had coffee and cake.

That's how it was that Joel discovered Miss Thompson sitting in a corner of the dining room chatting with Grandpa, and remembered that it was *her* voice he had heard in the living room before the show. It wasn't easy to recognize her, even now that he saw her. For she looked quite different from the busy person who played the piano so beautifully for the school assembly, and coached the Glee Club and encouraged students to play violin solos. She was wearing a pretty gray silk dress and sparkling blue beads around her neck; and she sat back lazily in the armchair, her eyes bright with fun. She held out her hand to Joel, smiling gaily.

"Hello, Joel," she said. "I've had a lovely time, and I want to thank you for it."

"I'm glad," said Joel shyly. He looked up at Grandpa, who nodded to him in encouragement. "Because . . . we had lots of fun too."

"I can see that!" she said. She shook hands with Grandpa and went to say good-by to Mother and Father.

"So you liked it, Grandpa?" said Joel to the guest of honor. But he didn't have to ask the question. Grandpa had been both surprised and pleased as he watched the stories come to life in a way he had never imagined.

As further evidence that he was pleased, on the following morning Grandpa took down the little rug Summer Sky had woven and the peace pipe of Wakanchara and gave them to Joel for his own room.

There was another sequel to Grandpa's show. In school, Monday morning, Miss Keegan beckoned Joel and said: "Miss Thompson would like to see you. In her classroom."

Joel felt his heart jump. Miss Thompson, aside from her music, was the fifth-grade teacher. As he went along the corridor, Joel wondered what she could want of him. He was less shy than he used to be; but he still felt very awkward at having to enter a class full of older boys and girls, all of whom would turn their heads to stare at him.

"Well, I'll just have to go through with it," Joel told himself, hand on the doorknob. He made himself turn it. Then he pushed the door open.

CHAPTER TWELVE

THE BIG SHOW

It wasn't so bad, after all. For hardly had the eyes turned on him than he noticed that Sally was there too, seated beside Miss Thompson's desk.

"Come in, Joel," the teacher called to him pleasantly. Soon he was sitting in a chair next to Sally's.

"Mr. Adams has put me in charge of Jewish Day," Miss Thompson said in her soft, clear voice, which didn't seem to reach beyond her desk, now that she wanted just Sally and Joel to hear it. "And I'd like to have you give your three little plays in assembly. They'd make a lovely show for Jewish Day. What do you think?"

Joel was so surprised that for a moment he couldn't speak at all. He could only look at Miss Thompson and wonder if he was dreaming. How else could it happen that a teacher—a grown-up lady—should be speaking to him as if he, too, were grown-up? He felt the blood creeping up to his forehead. "Oh—I couldn't," he whispered at last.

"Why not?" she coaxed. "What's the trouble?" Her eyes sparkled and she smiled. In his mind Joel remembered her as the lady in the gray silk dress with the bright beads around her neck. It became easy to talk to her.

"Well, you see, we were just having fun . . ." he began. "I mean it started that way."

"It *was* fun. Perfectly wonderful!" She laughed softly and glanced at Sally, who nodded.

"We weren't doing it for any reason—" He stopped, surprised at himself. "Yes—we were, too. We wanted to please Grandpa."

"And now you'll please Mr. Adams, and me, and the whole school," said Miss Thompson as if she believed every word she was saying.

Joel caught his breath. "Oh no! That's different," he pleaded.

"Only because you're nervous," she said. "Of course this won't be a little group of people in your own garden. This is a bigger audience, mostly children. Saturday the audience was mostly grownups. Yet you weren't afraid of *them!*"

"No," he said. "But they wanted to come. They . . . they were interested."

"Don't you think the children will be interested? The Jewish children will be glad to know what Jewish people have done in our country's history, for love of freedom. And it will be good for the others to know it too. Just as you and Sally will be watching the shows on Irish Day and Italian Day and Negro Day and Polish Day. *We* want to know about the other people here, don't we?" Joel nodded. "Well, they want to know about *you*."

Joel no longer thought of the several hundred eyes that would gaze at him from the auditorium. A warm, wonderful excitement was rising in him. He looked at Sally. "You think we can?"

"Sure we can," Sally said calmly. "It will go off beautifully."

"And I'll be right with you, all the time," said Miss Thompson. "I'll be only too glad to help out, or to get you anything you want. Just ask me!"

She looked so pleased that Joel felt happy too. There was a new thrill in looking forward to Brotherhood Week.

They rehearsed after school, either in Miss Thompson's room or in the auditorium.

"There's just one thing I'd like to suggest," said Miss Thompson to Joel before the first rehearsal. "When one actor takes more than one part in a scene, it's perfectly all right. You and Sally and your friends all know one another and understand what's going on, because you've acted the parts so often. But when you act it for a larger audience, it might confuse them to see one person acting two different characters in the same scene."

"Yes, but the gang isn't big enough for each one to take just one part," said Joel.

"Exactly. But here we have other boys and girls

who would like to be in the plays. Let them take the extra parts."

"Fine!" Sally exclaimed, looking over the youngsters who came forward eagerly.

"Pick them out yourselves." Miss Thompson sat down at her desk. "Joel and Sally will decide. I'll come in only if there's a fight."

The children laughed.

Everything went smoothly. Leo didn't mind when a taller boy was chosen for the part of John Brown. He could still be Jacob Benjamin, one of the two friends who went with August Bondi to join the camp of the Free Staters.

When all parts were given out, there were still twelve children left over. They looked disappointed.

"Don't worry," said Joel. He told the boys they could be sailors on the ships of Columbus, and Winnebagoes in the Indian story, and volunteers in the camp of John Brown. "And, when we're acting, if anyone can think of something good to say, say it. If we like it, that will be your part," he added.

"Good," said Miss Thompson. "Then the girls can be ladies attending Queen Isabella, and Winnebago squaws in the Indian story."

"That will make it more natural," Sally exclaimed, clasping her hands for joy.

At rehearsals the new actors got used to their

parts. Costumes were tried on. Miss Thompson brought a white satin gown for Sylvia which went beautifully with the red robe Sally had made. It came down over Sylvia's feet and made her look much taller.

Best of all was the lovely music Miss Thompson played for them. It came in just at the right moments. A stately march for the King and Queen. The stormy beating of waves against the Admiral's flagship, in the lonely night, before the mutineers entered ordering Columbus to turn back. A sweet, sad accompaniment to the song of Summer Sky.

"Swing Low, Sweet Chariot," for the camp of John Brown. . . .

Joel felt a warm glow in his heart at the very first notes. The music made you *ready* to act.

Brotherhood Week arrived. Irish Day was over.

Monday night, just a day and a half before his own show was to go on, Joel was awakened by a terrible toothache. A sharp pain dug into his lower jaw on the left side, and made him shiver from head to foot. It stabbed again and again, and wouldn't stop.

Sitting up in bed, Joel rocked back and forth with one hand on the aching cheek and the other gripping his elbow. But that didn't make it any better. He lay down again, rolling his head from side to side. He burrowed into the pillow, hoping it would ease the pain; but if anything, that made it worse.

Joel decided to get up. He switched on the light and looked at himself in the small mirror above his desk. His left cheek was swollen and his mouth was pulled to one side. He knew he was losing his baby teeth. The front teeth, upper and lower, had loosened themselves and fallen out, and the teeth from the second set had grown in, without any trouble. Why, all of a sudden, should he have this toothache? And just when he had been feeling so fine!

Another thought made him even more miserable. How could he act in the show on Jewish Day, looking like this?

Joel groaned as he thought how happy he had been only that morning—and all day, up to now. It was all he could do not to cry out loud.

But he wasn't a baby. He didn't have to wake the whole house. Perhaps if he took some cold water in his mouth it would stop the pain.

Very quietly Joel went into the bathroom and switched on the light. But he had just closed the door behind him when the handle turned and Mother's voice asked softly: "What's the matter, Joel?"

He had tried not to wake her. But what a relief it was, to let her in! "I didn't want to dis-turb you, Mom," he wept.

"You didn't disturb me at all." She turned his face to the light. A tear trickled down his swollen cheek and fell on her hand. "I've learned to sleep with one eye open," she said. "It's probably a back tooth. I don't believe I can even reach it with medicine. It will be too painful for you, if I try. We'll have to treat it from the outside. Come downstairs with me."

In the kitchen she set an iron skillet on the gas stove and emptied a bag of salt into it, stirring it to heat it evenly. "This is an old-fashioned remedy," she said. "Grandmother used it on us, in emergencies; and it always helped." She poured the salt back into the soft white cotton bag, and wrapped it in a silk kerchief which she carefully tied around Joel's head so that the heat came against the swelling. Then she sat in the rocker and took him on her lap.

He wanted her to hold him, yet he was ashamed of being such a baby. He hid his eyes against her shoulder, and a sob burst from him.

Mother read his mind. "There's nothing to be ashamed of, son," she explained. "Even grownups need to be babied when they're sick. They have to let their mothers take care of them, and it doesn't make them any less brave or big. Things happen, sometimes, that are too much for you. Then it's good if you have your mother." She held him close and patted him lovingly.

"What will—I do—about Jewish Day?" he gasped.

"It isn't here yet," said Mother. "We'll get you better by then."

At the mere thought that this was possible, Joel stopped crying. Then, between the warm feeling that came from Mother, and the heat of the salt bag, he began to feel sleepy. The pain had almost ceased.

"I feel better now," he said.

"Then I'll make up a bed for you on the couch." She led the way to the living room, and laid out a folded sheet and a pillow and blanket. "Go to sleep," she said, "and I'll sit here a while, to make sure everything's all right."

"But I don't want the others . . ." Joel began.

Mother gave him an impatient look. Then she smiled. "Don't worry. Leave it to me." She sat near him with some darning to do. As she rocked, slowly and quietly, Joel became very drowsy and was soon asleep.

He woke up when the sky was beginning to grow light, but the house was still quiet. Nobody was stirring yet. He was feeling quite well.

Hardly had he gotten to his feet when Mother came in. She took away the bedding. No one would be able to tell that anything had gone wrong with him.

"Thanks, Ma!" Joel said in a tone full of gratitude.

After breakfast she said: "I think we'd better see the dentist. Especially if you'd like to make sure of being all right tomorrow."

The tooth wasn't aching any more, but Joel didn't trust that tooth. Suppose it should hurt again tonight? Or maybe his face would swell again tomorrow?

The dentist said: "It's an abscessed molar. It had better come out."

"Now?" Joel asked.

"If you're ready." Dr. Gross left it for Joel to decide.

Joel remembered what Father had said, while

working on something he didn't enjoy doing. "Might as well get it over with," said Joel casually.

At lunchtime it was pleasant to hear Mother telling how brave he had been. She gave him a note for Miss Keegan, explaining his absence.

On the way to school, when Sylvia asked him if she might see the tooth, and Joel fished it out of his pocket, she put her hand against her cheek and exclaimed: "My gracious, what a big one! Is it still bleeding?"

He shrugged. "It's nothing," he said. He was only too glad that he could take part in the final rehearsal and be ready for tomorrow's performance.

It was the last nervous moment before the show began. King Ferdinand and Queen Isabella were ready, at one side of the platform. Joel, as Luis de Torres, waited at the opposite side, just back of Jerry, in the Admiral's cloak and oilcloth boots. Joel felt hot and shaky. The children out front made a rustling sound that died away to complete silence.

Music burst out—music that prepared you to hear about a great event in world history. Joel's heart lifted, and he was full of a happy impatience.

The plays began. Joel lived through every story again, as it was acted. He felt as if all this had happened to him. He wasn't surprised, now, that his schoolmates out front also found it real and shared the excitement.

Of course some things went wrong, but they seemed only to increase the audience's pleasure. In the Indian story the tent collapsed behind Summer Sky and the chieftains. Everyone laughed.

Joel said to his actors: "Let's push it back, out of the way, and start over again, without it."

"That's right!" said a girl out front. "Don't let it throw you!" shouted some boys. "Begin again!"

They began the scene again, and it went off better than ever.

When August Bondi and his two friends were making their first appearance before John Brown, the boy who was Theodore Weiner forgot his part. He froze up suddenly, and couldn't speak.

Joel said encouragingly, and loud enough for everyone to hear: "You ought to say something like: 'John Brown, we want to join you. We want Kansas to be a free state. We don't want any slaves anywhere!' "

The boy came to life. He said: "Captain Brown, we like what you're doing; and we've come to help. We want to fight on your side, so Kansas will be free. We want this to be a free country!"

"*Good!*" said Joel, and the audience applauded.

There were no more accidents. The last play went on to a fine finish.

Mr. Adams came up onto the platform and led the applause. Miss Thompson stepped forward, leading Sally, in the make-up of the fugitive slave,

and Joel, still wearing the palm-leaf hat and patched-together uniform of August Bondi. More applause and cheers. Then the other actors on the platform, unable to hold back their happiness, joined in the clapping. Joel suddenly became shy. He broke away and ran off stage.

Everyone laughed again.

At the end of the school day Joel and Sally were carrying home the red damask tablecloth and some of the other things they had brought to help with the show. Turning a corner, they saw that Alex was strolling a block or two ahead, with some other high-school boys.

Stewy Bleeker, now in the eighth grade at Joel's school, ran shouting past Joel and Sally without noticing them. Alex stopped, to wait for him.

"How was the show?" Alex called out.

"Pretty good!" said Stewy. His voice came clearly to Joel and Sally. "I thought I'd die laughing, though. Here was the tent, with the Indian chiefs and a powwow going on. And, right in the middle, the tent collapses! They kept their nerve, though. Your kid brother says: 'Push it back out of the way, and start over.' And so they did. You gotta give them credit for nerve."

They didn't hear what Alex said to that. But Stewy burst out again: "You can't tell me it was all thought up by the kids themselves! G'wan! Who're you kidding!"

Now they could hear Alex. "The idea," he replied firmly, "was thought up by the kid himself. And no grownups helped him, either. My kid brother, Joel."

A thrill of pleasure ran through Joel as he heard Alex stand up for him. There was such pride in his big brother's voice it made Joel's heart throb with gratitude.

Gee! I wish, Joel thought, I wish I could do something for Alex! I wish I could pay him back, talking up for me like that. Gosh! If I only could!

CHAPTER THIRTEEN

CATCHING UP

Joel's chance to do something for Alex came along very soon—just a few days after Brotherhood Week, in fact.

Supper was over. Joel, who had been roller-skating that afternoon, was already working out his arithmetic examples at the dining-room table, for he wanted to get out of doors again before bedtime. He was just wondering at the fact that six times six works out to the same as three times twelve when he heard Alex's voice, loud and troubled. The word "scrapbook" caught Joel's attention. He looked up.

"Where is it? Anybody see my scrapbook?" Alex asked.

Sally, busy with the maps she was drawing, shook her head.

"No," said Phil. "Maybe you took it upstairs."

"But I haven't been upstairs since I got home," Alex argued. Still they both went to look.

In a minute Joel heard them clattering down again. "Not there," said Phil.

Mother had come in from the kitchen. "Where did you put it when you came into the house?" she asked.

"Right here." Alex jerked his head toward Mother's sewing machine. When it was not in use they were allowed to put their books on its flat top, rather than clutter the sideboard.

"Unh-unh." Joel shook his head. "I saw you put your books down, Alex. The scrapbook wasn't there. I'd know it. It's a lot bigger than the others."

Joel and Alex were staring anxiously at the lace cover on the machine top as if, just by the strength of their wish, the large, square book must appear on it. At last Alex said miserably: "Then I must have lost it outside."

"Weren't you playing games before you came indoors?" Mother suggested. "Take a flashlight, and look for it where you put your other books down. You may have forgotten to pick it up."

"Could be!" shouted Alex. He was already at the front door, with Phil close behind him. Joel scrambled after his brothers.

They ran to the high fence along the embankment in which their street ended. "This is where we dropped our jackets and the books, I'm sure," said Alex, staring down at the near corner. They searched along the entire length of the fence.

They could see nothing but dead leaves and bits of paper, so they returned home.

"Now why didn't you bring the books in, first thing!" sighed Mother, looking almost as upset as the boys were.

"Stewy was all wound up. He's going to be a baseball pro, and he always wants me to catch for him. So I just put them down for a minute," Alex cried. "Who'd ever think it could disappear?"

"Wait a moment." Philip said suddenly. "Maybe one of the boys picked it up by mistake, with his own books."

"Good idea!" Alex caught eagerly at the new hope. "We'll go and ask them."

Joel followed. He couldn't wait to hear that the book was found!

Father was waiting for them, serious but very kind.

Alex told about their unsuccessful search. He threw himself down on a chair, looking miserable. "I was just going to type the last two poems tonight and paste them up," he groaned. "I'd be finished 'way ahead of time. And now, look!"

"When do you have to hand it in to your teacher?" Father asked.

"Not until next week."

"Well. You typed carbon copies of the poems. You'll have time to make up another book."

"But it won't look so good," Alex whispered. "And without the pictures—"

"Oh-h-h!" Joel moaned. "Up the airy mountain" wouldn't look or sound nearly so well without the picture of the waterfall he had found!

"Don't take it so hard, son." Father put his hand on Alex's shoulder. With a half-smile he added: "I hope nothing worse ever happens to you."

But Alex was silent. He couldn't cheer up.

Father sat down opposite him. "Think back," Father said. "Was there any other time when you put the books down? Did you stop to buy candy or ice cream?"

"Yes." Alex lifted his head. "Across the way from school. And I remember, too, I put my books on a bench in the schoolyard, while I tied my shoelaces. Maybe the scrapbook's there. Or maybe the caretaker found it!" His face was shining again. "Thanks, Dad!" he cried. "Come on, Phil!"

They raced away. As Joel quickly followed, Mother called out: "Joel, stay here!"

Joel remained at the gate, gripping it tightly. With all his heart he wanted to follow his brothers, but there was no mistaking the firmness in Mother's tone.

"What's the matter with Alex?" said a voice at Joel's side. "What's he sore about?"

It was Sylvia. She was hanging on the garden gate on her side of the fence.

Somehow it was a relief to talk. Joel said: "He's

lost his scrapbook, the one he has to have for English class next week."

"What's it look like?"

"It's a big book. Square. Like this." With his hands about ten or twelve inches apart, he showed her the width of it; then the length of the pages from top to bottom.

"Was it black?" she asked quickly.

"Yes." Then: "How'd you know?" Joel stared at her.

Sylvia came close to the fence. "I saw Stewy with a book like that. He hid it in his garden—in the hollow tree."

"Wow!" Joel gasped. He flung the gate back and dashed along the sidewalk to the Bleekers' garden.

The house was dark, except for a light in the hallway. It looked as if no one was home. Softly Joel unlatched the garden gate, pushed it back and stole quietly across the lawn. Here was the tree stump, all covered with ivy that hid the big hollow on the side toward the house.

Joel plunged his arms in, feeling carefully along the walls of the hollow. His heart was thumping against his ribs. If he could only find the scrapbook! If he could do this for Alex! Yet the roots of his hair were prickling with fear. A door slammed inside the house. Someone was coming downstairs. . . .

Joel brought his arms lower. Dead leaves were

piled here. Then his hands met the hard covers of the book. He drew it out with a thrill of triumph. It was dusty from the leaves, and spotted with dew. But he had it!

He got to his feet and ran.

The door opened and a tall figure leaped down from the porch and, with one long stride, stood between Joel and the gate. It was Stewy, big as a grown man.

Dodging, Joel made a dash for the sidewalk. But Stewy had only to turn on his heel and stretch out those long arms. Joel was caught.

Panting, Joel dropped to his knees and bent himself double to protect the book. It was useless. With one hand Stewy wrenched it from his grasp.

Joel jumped up. "That's my brother's book!" he yelled.

"He's got enough books!" Stewy growled. His chin stuck out. There was a mean, sulky look on his face. "He's always got his nose in a book!"

"That's none of your business," Joel shouted. His hand was on the back of his neck, where Stewy had hurt him in snapping his head backwards.

"It is, too, and I'll tell you why!" Stewy raged. "If not for the books, he'd be a good fellow. He's a swell catcher! He'd make a good addition to the team. Instead he wastes his time fixing up a scrapbook! Poetry!" He flung it away on the grass.

Joel gasped. The precious book had fallen open. By the light of the street lamp he could see the tiger picture—the green eyes and snapping teeth.

Joel ran to it. Stewy took one step forward, aiming a punch at Joel's face.

Joel stopped. With that terrible, big fist an inch from his nose, he blinked rapidly. He shrank together as if, for once, he wished he were smaller. But he didn't retreat. He didn't draw back an inch.

Meanwhile thoughts were whizzing through his mind. He was frightened. Suppose he ran away. He could still tell Alex where the book was. But

Stewy might destroy it. Joel simply couldn't leave.

He straightened up. "So what?" he argued. "If my brother likes poetry, hasn't he got the right? You like baseball. Suppose you made a scrapbook out of baseball players. How would you like it if someone swiped it and wouldn't give it back?"

Stewy put both hands in his pockets. Joel took a wary step toward the book. The big boy stood motionless. The mean look was gone from his face. He seemed busy with his thoughts.

Joel stole across the grass and gathered up the scrapbook. Hugging it close, in cautious dashes he got past Stewy and out through the gateway.

At that moment Alex and Phil were coming up the block, tired and heavyhearted from their fruitless search.

"I've got it!" Joel shouted, running to meet them. "Here it is! Stewy had it." Sylvia flew behind him, chattering at the top of her voice.

"Oh no!" Alex gasped for sheer joy, giving way at the knees and pretending to faint, with his arms around Phil's shoulders.

Philip held him up, smiling. Then, punching him fondly in the ribs, he said: "Get off. You weigh a ton."

They came up to the Bleekers' house. Stewy, leaning on the gate, was grinning awkwardly. "Maybe I'll make myself a scrapbook," he said. "I got stacks of baseball mags." Turning away, he strolled indoors.

They hurried toward their own house. Sylvia skipped along beside them, hugging herself for glee. "You should've been here, Alex," she shouted, determined to make herself heard. "You ought've seen him, Phil! The way he talked back to Stewy! Joel's not afraid of anyone!"

"Yeah?" Phil smiled, pulling at her curls.

"Sylvia! *Come in!* It's long past your bedtime," her mother's voice called from an upstairs window.

"I gotta go." Abruptly she turned up the path to her house and ran.

"S'long, Sylvia! Thanks!" Joel cried gaily.

In the house everyone was overjoyed, and very pleased with Joel.

"Boy! Am I thirsty!" he exclaimed.

"We'll all have some ginger ale," said Mother. "Sally, get the glasses."

Alex threw his arms around Joel and hugged him. "You're a pal, Joel!" he said. He ruffled Joel's hair. It wasn't the old, condescending pat on the head.

Sunday morning Alex said to Joel: "Want to come with us to the museum?"

"Yippee!" Joel shouted. "Just ask me. Only ask me!" Then he quieted down. "I don't have any money for carfare."

"Another time we can go Dutch treat. This time I'm paying for you," Alex smiled. Joel didn't know which made him happier, the fact that Alex was taking him or the words "Another time . . ."

Mother packed lunch for them in shoeboxes, neatly wrapped. They were calling out good-bys and were ready to start when Father came out into the hallway.

He looked them over, with a smile in his eyes. "What's the show at the Hayden Planetarium?" he asked Alex.

"A Trip to the Moon," replied Alex sadly, for he knew they had no money for it.

"Well," said Father, "as long as this is Joel's first visit to the Museum of Natural History, we have to do it in style. You can take that trip."

Father gave Alex money for their admission to the planetarium. "Wow!" the boys shouted. Sally kissed Father.

They were off.

They had decided not to eat their lunch until one o'clock. But somehow, as soon as they arrived at the museum building, they felt hungry. So they went into the park, where the red and golden leaves were glistening in the mild sunshine, and had a real picnic. There was an egg and lettuce sandwich, a salmon sandwich and a nut-bread sandwich for each of them, plus cup cakes and oranges.

When they entered the museum, Joel looked around him awe-stricken. "Now we can't try to see everything," Alex informed him. "That would take years and years! But we'll pick out a few things we think you'd like." Joel nodded, flattered at the special attention.

In the Hall of the Pacific Northwest they looked at the huge, seagoing canoe made out of a hollow tree trunk. Life-sized models of Indians were seated on the thwarts, rowing. Others were grouped around their chief. There were medicine men with strange, frightening masks; and one dressed up like a bear, with claws and a long, toothy muzzle.

From there they went up one flight of stairs to the African Hall. A lifelike group of elephants seemed to be marching down its center. Joel and Sally were specially charmed with the baby elephant that, sheltered amid the great beasts, curled his little trunk around his mother's.

Along the walls, in natural settings that imitated their homes and reproduced the brilliant African sunshine, were figures of lifelike animals. Gorillas, tall giraffes and playful zebras near a waterhole, a family of lions, handsome deerlike creatures with graceful horns and funny names.

"Here's the bongo," said Alex, introducing Joel.

"And there's the greater kudu," laughed Sally.

"Come along now," said Alex. "Another time you'll see the Asian animals, and the enormous fishes. But you don't want to get too tired. You can walk miles in this place."

Though Joel would gladly have stayed longer in the African Hall, he knew that he must do what the

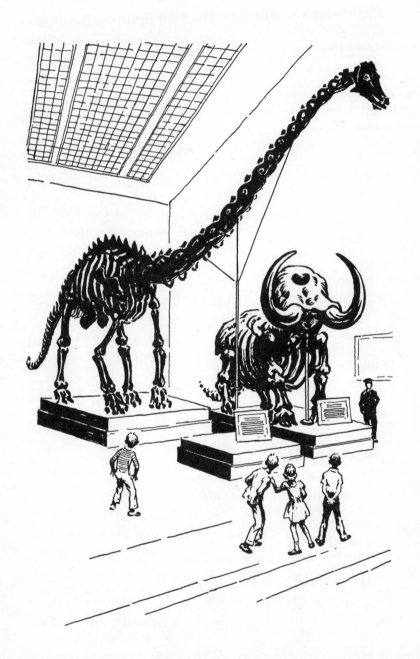

others wished, and not be a nuisance. "Another time . . ." came pleasantly to his mind.

"Now we'll see the dinosaurs," Sally promised him.

"Sally's afraid of them," Phil teased.

"No, I'm not," she protested. "I only said I wouldn't like to meet one in the dark."

Joel gasped at sight of the tremendous skeletons.

"They lived on the earth about forty million years before there were any human beings. This one ate other dinosaurs." Alex pointed out a monster that sat up on its hind legs like a kangaroo, and used its forepaws to hold its prey while the big toothy jaws in its small head opened to devour it! Its height was that of four tall men, and a heavy, pointed tail made up half its length. Joel could hardly tear himself away from the sights he saw here.

Then they went to the planetarium. They stood on scales that showed them how much more they would weigh on great planets like Jupiter, and how much less on the moon. They waited in the Hall of the Sun, represented by a bright globe in the center of the ceiling. Around it circled the planets, each on its fixed path, at the proper distance from the sun—Mercury closest, then Venus, then the Earth with its moon, then Mars—and further out was wonderful Saturn with its rainbow rings and six moons; and Jupiter, with four moons.

Then came the best part of all. "Wait till you see!" Sally whispered as they filed into the circular auditorium and took their seats under the great dome. Soon it flashed with the likeness of the starry sky, and the lecturer's voice told them how they would set out on their imaginary flight to the moon.

Joel settled back in his chair. With a glad pattering of his heart he told himself this was the most wonderful day in all his life. It wasn't because of the ride and the picnic. It wasn't because of the museum and the planetarium.

The most blissful thought was this: he was catching up with his brothers at last.